September

I'm so excited I can barely write. A proper, real fortune teller gave me some amazing news today. I was at the summer fair near our house when I saw this funny little red-and-white tent with a sign outside it that said 'Fortune Telling'. I peeped inside and saw a strange old man sitting all hunched up in a green camping chair. He looked up at me then pointed his bony finger towards the chair opposite him. I stared at him for a moment, noticing that one of his eyes was like a shiny white marble. I wondered if I should run.

'Sit down,' he said in a croaky voice.

3

I crept in and lowered myself into the chair. He tapped an old tin can on a low table. There was a clank as I dropped my coin in.

'Hmmmmmmmmmmmmmmmm,' he said, his eyes shut tight. I sat there for about a minute before he spoke again. 'I see good things for you.' He stopped and took a huge raspy breath in. 'You will have a big win during the next year, but you have to make it happen.'

'OK,' I said, waiting for more. The old man stood up slowly then, taking the coin from the tin, stumbled out of the tent. I sat there for a while wondering if he was coming back. In the end I left and went to look for my best friend Holly. I met her by the ghost train as we'd arranged and we had a great time at the fair. We spun in the waltzers until we were dizzy, we got candyfloss, and I even won a sponge bag on the tombola.

'There, you've had your win now,' said Holly, as I looked inside the bag.

'It can't be this,' I said, as I opened and closed the zip a few times. 'I've got a feeling that old man was a real fortune teller.' I was so excited I tried to do a cartwheel and ended up on the floor giggling. The words 'but you have to make it happen' swirled around my brain.

Maggie Moore
Wants to Win

By Firna Rex Shaw

For Sheila

First Print Edition
Copyright 2013

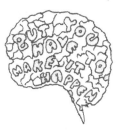

Thursday, September 6th

School starts again in four days and I can't wait to see the girls. I've got three best friends – Holly, Mandy and Sarah.

Mandy always goes on holiday to America during the summer break. She comes back with all these amazing new things, like stationery, key rings and clothes. I want to go to America and go shopping, but I don't think it will ever happen as Mum prefers cheap holidays. I went on holiday to the forest this year, the usual camping trip with my mum, dad and younger brother Joppin. I didn't get to go to any shops at all, but my mum did get me a gift, which she wrapped up nicely. It even had a small silver bow on the top. When I opened it, I found out it was a pine cone. It was just like the thousands of pine cones all around our tent, and like the ten or so that were my under sleeping bag the night before.

Friday, September 7th

Oh no! I'm hiding in the bathroom because I have a major problem.

I have a spot.

It's right above the middle of my top lip. When I look in the mirror my eyes are drawn straight to the big, red, glowing spot.

I've tried to cover it up with Mum's skin-coloured powder and her skin-coloured cream. I've even tried wet toilet paper, which I licked and stuck over it. (It was peach-coloured so I thought it might work. It didn't.) School starts in three days and I really hope it's gone before then.

Monday, September 10th
FIRST DAY BACK
The spot is still there, OH NO.

When I got to school this morning, I saw Holly and Sarah straight away. Holly's hair was tied up in a messy bun, and Sarah had new glasses balanced on the end of her nose.

'Hi, Maggie,' they called, as they ran over to me. I would have been embarrassed about the spot, but I'd thought of this clever way to hide it by holding my finger over my top lip at all times. I did it so casually that it just looked like I was resting my finger there.

'Hi! How were your holidays?' I said through my other fingers. We then talked about the holidays for a while. During the conversation I noticed that Holly had started copying me. Her finger was also resting over her top lip. I don't even think she realized she was doing it. This was very good as it made the finger over the top lip look like a new trend.

'I'm here!' someone shouted behind us. We turned round to see Mandy entering the playground. Her blond hair looked very straight, like it had been ironed. She had this amazing new bag swinging on her shoulder. It looked like a huge red Converse trainer, complete with laces and a leather strap. She also had a plaster cast on her arm, which was covered in a fancy rainbow-covered sleeve thing. It looked really good.

'What happened?' asked Holly and me in unison as she joined us.

'Oh, my arm? I broke it in America. I fell on the stairs at the airport. We couldn't fly after that. We had to stay for another week, which meant more shopping for me,' she said, as she swung her bag around.

The bell went and we all rushed into our new classroom. I grabbed a seat next to Holly. Mr Nervel was standing at the front of the class. He's going to be our teacher for the year. This is not the best news because he's a very quiet man and he can't control the class. This means that some of the sillier boys like Jake and Peter will play up all the time.

Mr Nervel looked different to the last time I'd seen him before the holidays. I wasn't sure what it was, but then I noticed he'd grown a moustache. It was a very unusual moustache because the hair was very straight and parted in the middle.

So there we sat, Holly and me with our fingers over our top lips. Jake saw this and laughed before doing it too. Before long the whole class were sitting with their finger over their top lip. Mr Nervel looked very upset. He glanced at us then stood looking out of the window for a long time. Eventually, he rubbed his eyes and turned round to face the class.

'You can make fun of my moustache all you want but it won't upset me,' he said, his voice wavering.

Everyone removed their finger except me. (I couldn't remove mine or everyone would see the spot.) As I was sitting near the front Mr Nervel stared straight at me.

'You can't beat me,' he said in a very high voice. Then he rushed out.

We waited quite a long time but Mr Nervel didn't come back. Sarah went to get help, and after a long wait Mrs Foley, the head teacher, came in and did the lesson with us.

At playtime everyone crowded around Mandy, asking about her arm. I never realized that having an injury could cause so much excitement. Once the crowd had died down and it was just Holly, Sarah, Mandy and me, Mandy got out her boot bag from America and put it on the picnic table.

She opened it and lined up the new items she'd got on holiday:

A pack of smelly pencils (nice smells - except cinnamon)

Light-up hair slides that change colour every fourteen seconds

Seventeen novelty rubbers (all good shapes)
Nail art stickers that make your nails look like
computer chips

We all smelt the pencils, which were amazing. Mandy then gave us one pencil each. Mine was chocolate-scented – my very favourite smell so I was mega pleased.

At lunchtime I told Mandy and Sarah about the fortune teller saying that I would have a big win during the next year. Their eyes opened wide and we all came up with ideas as to what the win might be. It was decided that if anyone saw any interesting competitions or events with big prizes, I must enter.

Tuesday, September 11th

It turns out that Mr Nervel isn't going to be a teacher any more. He's left the school due to stress. Holly found out as her mum knows his wife. Apparently, Mr Nervel had been driven over the edge when the kids made fun of his moustache. Oh dear!

I've still got a spot but I've found the perfect way to cover it up. I found this small round plaster in Mum's make up bag. It's skin-coloured so you can't even tell I'm wearing it. RESULT!

Wednesday, September 12th

I found out today that we'll be getting a new teacher called Mr Winters. I know him a bit as he's done some supply teaching over the years. He's mega strict and demanding. Jake said he used to be in the army. We all trembled a little when we heard the news that he'll be starting next Monday.

Everyone rushed over to Mandy at playtime. They were all trying to feel the cast on her arm. She pulled back the sleeve and let everyone write on it. Peter asked if he could sign the small round plaster on my lip. I could feel my face flush as he lurched at me with a pen. I was shocked that he'd even noticed it, and I didn't move as he leant in and wrote something. Straight afterwards I rushed into the toilets and saw that the word 'POP' (for Peter Oliver Potter) was written on it in black pen. I immediately peeled the plaster off and went back outside. I reverted to holding my finger over my top lip.

Friday, September 14th

Over breakfast I scoured the local paper for competitions but there weren't any good ones. There was a 'Win a Toaster' competition, but I didn't want to waste my win on something we already have.

Peter arrived at school with a large sticker on his head. He said he'd cracked his head open and it was a plaster he'd got at the hospital.

'It looks very much like one of the address stickers my mum uses on her eBay packages,' I said to Holly, and she agreed.

At playtime Holly asked if she could sign Peter's plaster. He looked pleased.

'Yes, as long as you don't press too hard,' he said, giving her a felt tip pen.

Holly wrote 'I am pretending to have an injury' on the sticker. We tried not to laugh until we were safely in the girls' toilets.

Later on we saw Peter crying in the playground. It turned out that Jake had seen the sticker and, thinking that the plaster was fake, had pulled it off, revealing a line of stitches and a nasty-looking injury. Eeeeeeeeek!

Monday, September 17th
MR JEREMY WINTERS

Today was Mr Winters' first day. We all tiptoed into the classroom and sat down to wait for him. The door flew open and in he marched. He stood very upright at the front of the room and saluted. No one quite knew what to do. A few people saluted back but most people just giggled quietly.

'Good morning, class. I'm Mr Winters,' he said in a fast, posh voice. 'This year will be tough. You will work harder than you have ever worked before. You will fall into bed each night exhausted.' We all exchanged worried glances. He raised his eyebrows. 'You will also play hard. In October I am taking you into the countryside for a three-day trip where we will do outdoor activities.'

We all cheered.

'Along with the usual work, I am going to inject a bit of fun into the year by splitting the class into three teams. This will help us to achieve a competitive spirit.' He then ran about the room pointing at people while shouting 'one', 'two' or 'three'. I was a number three.

'Ones are in a team called Royalty, twos are in Mammals, and threes are in Woodlice,' he said, as he wrote the three team names on the whiteboard.

I was horrified to learn I was in team Woodlice. What was even worse was that Holly, Sarah and Mandy were all in Royalty. Quentin, the biggest show-off in the school, had his head in his hands so I guessed he was in Woodlice too.

Mr Winters explained that we're going to be in these teams all year and we'll collect team points in various ways. 'There will be a cup at the end of each term and a big prize at the end of the year for the winning team,' he said.

I hope my win isn't going to be a group win with bunch of Woodlice.

At lunchtime the girls were going on and on about being in team Royalty. They were linking arms and strutting around the playground. Later on they let me join in, but they said it was a bit strange for queens to be linking arms with woodlice.

Tuesday, September 18th

Today Mr Winters wore a whistle on a red string around his neck. He handed out maths sheets then blew the whistle when we had to begin. After twenty minutes he blew the whistle again when we had to stop. The whistle sounded awful, it was so loud and piercing it made our ears hurt. At playtime the girls and I had a talk about it and we decided that we had to get rid of that whistle somehow. We knew he took it off to go to the toilet as he's done that twice already.

'Let's get it and hide it,' said Holly. 'You know, when he goes to the loo.'

'Too risky,' said Sarah. 'We could get into trouble. He might think we stole it.'

'I've got an idea,' I said, suddenly leaping up. 'Let's block it up!'

Sarah looked up, chewing on her bottom lip. 'They'd know someone had done it on purpose. We could get into trouble.'

'Let's make it look like an accident then,' I said, a plan forming in my head. On the way back to the classroom I got some wet toilet paper and stuffed it into my pocket.

Just before lunch Mr Winters took the whistle off and put in on the desk as he headed to the toilet. As I sit near the front it was easy for me to get the whistle and stuff it with the wet toilet paper.

After lunch we rushed back into the classroom, eager to see what would happen with the blocked whistle. Mr Winters picked it up and put the string over his head. We all held our breath as he blew. There was complete silence. The whole class started laughing. Mr Winters blew his whistle again - silence. The class laughed louder and Mr Winters looked ready to explode.

Just then Mrs Foley, the head teacher, opened the door to see what all the laughing was about. In a moment of panic Mr Winters blew his whistle mega hard, his eyes nearly popping out of his head.

Suddenly the wet toilet paper flew out and landed with a huge splat on Mrs Foley's glasses. It remained there, completely covering one lens. We all became very quiet and still. Mr Winters froze and Mrs Foley walked away, closing the door behind her.

'Times tables test,' said Mr Winters, throwing maths sheets onto our tables. Once we'd begun writing our answers on the sheets he rushed out of the room, and we could hear him apologizing to Mrs Foley in the corridor.

Wednesday, September 19th

Mr Winters said that we're going to be doing cross-country on Friday. Oh no! I hate cross-country – freezing knees, stitches, slogging along out of breath. It doesn't sound like fun to me. What makes the whole thing even worse is that we're getting team points for it. The better we do, the more team points we get. Quentin leant over to me and said, 'You'd better not let Woodlice down.' I wonder if I can get out of it somehow.

Friday, September 21st
DREADED CROSS-COUNTRY DAY

Mandy is so smug because her broken arm means she doesn't have to do cross-country. She's allowed to sit at the hexagonal table outside the lunchroom and draw instead. She even brought her glitter pens in specially. I asked if I could stay in and keep her company, to which both Mr Winters and Quentin replied 'No.' I had one more plan up my sleeve though.

When we were getting changed, I found that I'd accidentally (on purpose) forgotten my running shorts. I went to tell Mr Winters the terrible news. What happened next was weird. It was almost as if he knew someone would forget. He reached into his pocket and pulled out a pair of boys' large red underpants with a white trim. 'I brought these just in case anyone forgot,' he said. He bundled them into my hand and blew his whistle. 'Don't just stand there, get them on.'

I looked at the red underpants and then I looked at him to see if he was joking. He blew the whistle again. This gave me the awful feeling that he was serious.

I scurried away, clutching the underpants in my hand. Holly and Sarah were in absolute hysterics when I showed them. Holly was bent over double, hardly able to breathe. I pulled the pants on over my own pants. They looked like a baggy red nappy. I heard the whistle again and we all jogged out, with me hiding behind Holly.

When everyone saw me, they all started laughing and pointing. We all scuttled over to the woods opposite the school. My cheeks were as red as the underpants.

'Let's all run together,' I said to Holly and Sarah.

'Not sure,' said Sarah. 'We may have to run ahead. Royalty has to win.'

Mr Winters talked us through the route then blew his whistle. Everyone shot off, with Mr Winters leading the way at the front. I shuffled along holding up the underpants. At one point they slipped right down so I had to stop for a minute to sort them out.

Because of my underpants problem I was right at the back. I turned a corner and suddenly I was my own. I couldn't see anyone at all. I hadn't listened to the route as I figured I'd just follow everyone else. I looked all around but there were about four different paths to choose from, all going in different directions. I knew the route would end where it began, as that was near the school, so I decided to hide behind a tree and wait for the others then sneak back into the crowd at the end of the race.

I squatted behind a tree and drew lines in the dusty soil with twigs before collecting tiny stones and making a little stone circle. It was actually quite fun. After a while I could hear the pitter-patter of footsteps and I got up ready to re-join the group by slipping in at the back. I was just looking out from behind the tree when Mr Winters saw me. I held my breath and froze.

'Keep going, Maggie, you're nearly the winner!' he shouted.

I started running back to where we started. Mr Winters then ran in behind me, followed by everyone else. Everyone was breathing heavily with their hands on their knees so I did too.

'Well done, Maggie! Wow, you are a great runner!' Mr Winters said between breaths. 'You even beat me.'

Holly and Sarah caught up with me as we all walked back to school. 'Well done, Maggie!' said Holly. 'You were so fast I didn't even see you.'

I couldn't believe that no one suspected a thing. When we got back to the classroom, Mr Winters got out three large pieces of paper. He had written the teams names on them. The top one said 'Royalty', one said 'Mammals', and one said 'Woodlice'. He put them up on the wall.

'Well done, Woodlice. Because of Maggie you get five points,' he said, putting five marks on the Woodlice poster. He drew sad faces on the other posters. Quentin gave me a thumbs up. 'And,' Mr Winters continued, 'I'm signing Maggie up for the cross-country team. If anyone else wants to join, the sign-up sheet will be on my desk.'

When I heard this, my teeth clamped together and I felt sweat on my forehead. I can't be in a cross-country team. I get tired just running across the playground. I tried to put it out of my mind.

Saturday, September 22nd

At breakfast I had a look at Dad's local paper and found a competition. The first prize was a trip to London for you and your family. The second prize was for Barry the Elephant to visit your school. I liked the idea of a trip to London. That would be great – going on the London Eye, a boat trip on the Thames, shopping in Harrods. The Barry the Elephant bit wasn't so good. Barry the Elephant is this silly TV show for toddlers. However, I was due a BIG win, which must mean first prize. I filled in my details and asked Mum to post it for me.

Monday, September 24th
BAD NEWS

Mr Winters asked me to stay back for a chat at the end of school. I waited in the classroom, biting my thumbnail. I was worried that he'd found out about me hiding behind a tree in cross-country or that he knew it was me who'd put toilet paper in his whistle.

He came in and sat down next to me.

'Maggie,' he said, rubbing his hands together, 'no one else has signed up for the cross-country so you will be the only one representing the school.' He tapped the whistle hanging around his neck a few times. 'And I will be your coach,' he added.

I struggled for words as the horror of the situation sank in.

'Oh!' I gasped, wondering how I was going to get out of it.

'The first race is in two weeks. I've already emailed your parents with the details,' he smiled, 'so get practising.'

'Right, um, bye then,' I said, getting up and rushing out. Holly, Mandy and Sarah were waiting for me outside.

'Well, come on then, what did he say?' asked Mandy.

'It was about the cross-country team. Hey, why don't you all sign up? It'll be fun.'

'What? Gasping about on a ghastly field with Mr Winters blowing his whistle at me? No way,' said Sarah.

Holly linked my arm. 'I would join but I can't,' said Holly. 'I've got a sore foot.' She started limping. I went home.

Mum had made me some buns to celebrate my being selected for the cross-country team. She said she was coming along to watch my first race. She'd even printed out Mr Winters' email and attached it to the fridge with her special piggy magnets.

Tuesday, September 25th

A while ago Mr Winters said that the class team (out of Royalty, Mammals and Woodlice) with the most points at the end of the year would get a prize. Today he told us that the prize would be a trip to The Big Apple. Mandy leant over to me and whispered, 'That's New York, in America.' I looked at the Woodlice sheet with its five points and decided that Woodlice could win. A trip to America would be brilliant. It was a shame I wouldn't be able to go with my friends but it would still be very, very good.

When I got home, I looked up 'The Big Apple' on the computer, and yes, it is a nickname for New York! YIPPEE!

Wednesday, September 26th

Only ten days until the cross-country race. I'm getting very worried about it. I just hope there's a big tree to hide behind.

Tuesday, October 1st

BUDDY SYSTEM

'You are each going to be a role model,' said Mr Winters this morning. 'You will help a younger child to settle into school and guide them through their first year.'

So everyone in our class became a buddy to a four or five-year-old child in the reception class. Pairs of names were pulled out of a hat just before playtime.

Holly got little Mary.

Mandy got Bob.

Sarah got Emily.

And I got someone called Riley.

'Well,' said Mr Winters, slapping name stickers on everyone, 'no time like the present. Let's go and meet our buddies.'

We all went into the reception playground. It was cold, and steam poured from our mouths as we rubbed our gloved hands together. We scoured the sea of little children, who also wore name stickers, looking for our buddies. Holly, Mary and Sarah found theirs almost straight away. They were chatting and playing with them. I was anxious to find Riley and I searched all the corners of the playground.

Then I saw a small boy looking at me. He had scruffy hair and a very long coat. I walked over to him and looked at his name sticker. Yes, it was Riley.

'Shall we play a game?' I asked nicely. He walked away from me.

Quentin and his buddy came over. 'You'd better follow him. We might get Woodlice points if we make our buddies happy,' he said. I sighed and followed Riley around the playground. Eventually, he stopped walking and we stood in silence for the whole playtime. It was the first time I'd ever been relieved to hear the bell ringing for lessons.

When we got back to our classroom, Mr Winters explained that next Monday we were going to interview our buddies. We have to find out what stories they like reading and then we'll be making them a book. If they like their book, we'll get a point for our team. Oh dear! I hope Riley starts talking soon.

Mr Winters came over to have a word with me just at the end of playtime.

'Good news regarding Saturday,' he said.

'Oh yes, the cross-country race,' I replied, not sounding too enthusiastic.

'I've got Tim Peters, an Olympic coach, coming to watch you. I've told him about your potential and he's very interested to see you run.'

'Oh!' I said, looking around for my friends. 'OK,' I said slowly, my heart pounding in my chest. I needed a plan before Saturday.

Wednesday, October 2nd
Oh no, the cross-country race is in three days!

Thursday, October 3rd
Oh no, the cross-country race is in two days!

Friday, October 4th

One day to go until the cross-country race! I've come up with a couple of ideas. My best plan is to hide behind a tree and my back-up plan is to pretend to have an injury during the race. Not sure exactly what to do yet. I'm going to wait and see tomorrow.

Saturday, October 5th
CROSS-COUNTRY RACE NEWS

Well, Mum woke me up early. We had a big breakfast then drove to the race. When I got there, I was shocked to see it was a huge field with hardly any trees. There was one in the far corner that had possible hiding potential.

It was cold with light drizzle, and I shivered and rubbed my arms as a sheet of plastic with the number seventy-three was safely pinned on me.

We saw Mr Winters and another man marching over in red tracksuits.

'Maggie, meet Tim Peters, Olympic coach,' said Mr Winters.

'I've heard a lot about you,' said Tim, offering his hand. I shook it and smiled awkwardly.

'Let's warm up then,' said Mr Winters. He started stretching. I joined in, as did Tim. It was rather embarrassing because Mum joined in too and added strange stretching noises.

After our warm-up we all made our way over to the start line and I joined the other hundred kids who were also in the race. The race co-ordinator told us to go right round the field, then through a gate into another field, round that one, and then back to the start. This was quite good news because the tree was halfway round the first field. I figured I could hide there but I hadn't figured out how to get back without being seen.

Suddenly, a large bang filled the air. I covered my head and dropped to the ground. All the other children started running. I got up and started running along at the back, heading for the tree. When I got there, I left the path and sat behind the tree. I found a nice stick and was busy stripping the bark off it, enjoying revealing the inner shiny stick. I was so busy with the stick that I almost forgot about the race. Then I heard a whistle followed by a familiar voice.

'Come on, come on!' shouted Mr Winters. He'd run after me and he was now standing in front of me frowning. I didn't look at him as I got up. Tim was there too, running on the spot. 'Step it up a gear,' said Tim.

'I think I've hurt my foot,' I said, waggling it around.

'Run through the pain,' said Mr Winters. I got up and carried on with a slow jog. By this time I was miles behind everyone else. I jogged along panting as Mr Winters and Tim shouted things into the wintry air.

'You only get out what you put in!' barked Mr Winters.

'Heroes are brave!' shouted Tim.

'A winner never quits and a quitter never wins!' shouted Mr Winters. This was a particularly strange encouragement as I was definitely not going to win. In fact, I was so slow that when we got to the finish line, everyone else had gone home.

'Well done for trying,' said Mum, giving me a hug.

I heard Mr Winters saying that he was sorry to Tim Peters, who didn't even say goodbye to me as he went off.

There was just me, Mum and Mr Winters left and I looked up anxiously, worried I'd be in trouble. I did have one good thought, which was that I probably wouldn't be asked to join the next race.

'You need to do a lot more practising before the next race,' said Mr Winters.

My heart sank. Luckily, the next race isn't for a month so I have a while to come up with a plan.

Monday, October 7th
BUDDY DAY

We met up with our buddies today. We all went into the reception playground carrying notepads and pencils. We were meant to ask them what kind of stories they like. I went up to Riley.

'What kind of stories do you like?' I asked.

Riley just walked away. Quentin saw this and came up to me.

'You'd better find out. You've got to get a point for the Woodlice,' he said.

'I will, I will,' I said. I'd forgotten that we would get team points for this project so I went up to Riley again. He walked away and I ended up following him around again.

In literacy this afternoon everyone was busy writing story plans. They all had loads of notes about their buddies' interests. Some even had drawings. I decided to make something up. I remember Joppin talking about a funny character called the bogeyman. I wasn't sure what it was but it sounded good, so I started planning a story about that.

Story Plan

A bogeyman lives in a puddle.
He grabs people as they walk past the puddle.
He pulls them through the puddle into the bogeyman world.

30

I was really excited about my story and wrote until my hand hurt. The stories have to be finished and illustrated by next Monday when we'll give them to our reception buddies. The title of mine is *Bogeyman Will Get You*.

At lunchtime I asked the others what their stories were about. Holly's writing a story about a fairy who's looking for a cookie. Sarah's is about a horse that can talk, and Mandy's is about a toy train. 'Poor you having to write about bogeymen,' said Mandy. They didn't realize it was all my own brilliant idea.

Wednesday, October 9th

We carried on with our stories yesterday, and today in art we did some illustrations. I did some amazing bogeyman pictures. I wasn't really sure what one looked like so I just guessed.

Jake got in trouble with Mr Winters today. He kept holding his nose while saying Peter had passed wind. He had to stand in the corridor for thirty minutes. 'Wind' is the word that most of the boys in our class use to mean the gas produced in your tummy when you eat too many beans.

BLARNEY HALL

Our residential outward bounds trip to Blarney Hall is in two weeks. We'll be sleeping in dormitories in a big house, and during the daytime we'll be doing all sorts of activities like canoeing, rock climbing and hiking. We'll be there for three days... EXCITING!

Thursday, October 10th

Today at playtime the girls and I looked over the fence into the reception playground. It was busy with all the little kids running around playing. Little Mary ran over and held hands with Holly through the fence. Emily came over and Sarah told her about the talking horse story. They both jumped up and down with huge grins on their faces. I looked for Riley. I saw him standing on his own watching a large group of boys playing together.

Friday, October 11th

We finished making our books today. We made covers and stapled them together in the middle. Mine actually looks like a proper book.

Saturday, October 12th

Mum, Dad, Joppin and I went to town today. We got some outdoor clothes for me to take to Blarney Hall. I got two pairs of tracksuit trousers, a waterproof coat and some black trainers. Only nine days to go.

Monday, October 14th
BUDDY DAY

We all got out the books we'd made ready to take them to the reception playground. I was a bit nervous as I didn't know if Riley would like my book. Holly, Sarah and Mandy had all said it was gross. I thought it was funny but I had no idea what Riley was interested in.

There were squeals of excitement as we entered the playground. Most of the buddies ran over to get their books. I couldn't find Riley for ages. I looked all around for him and in the end I found him sitting on the floor behind the toy shed all on his own. I sat down next to him.

'I've got your book,' I said. He didn't reply. 'Have a look. It took me ages to make it,' I said, holding it out to him. He grabbed it, got up, and ran away, holding it tightly.

All around the playground the kids were reading away, showing each other their books and chatting to their buddies. I looked for Riley and was pleased to see he was looking inside the bogeyman book. There was no obvious expression on his face so I still wasn't sure if he liked it. I decided to find Holly. She was reading the fairy story to little Mary. Mary was smiling and saying how good it was. I played with Holly and Mary for a while. At the end of playtime I noticed Riley was with someone. A boy in a red coat had gone over to him.

'Let's see it,' said the boy in the red coat. 'It looks good.' Riley showed him the book and they looked at it together. 'Let's play bogeyman,' said the boy.

'OK,' said Riley very quietly, and he started running around. As the bell went, Riley looked at me and smiled. It was a small smile, but definitely a smile.

Wednesday, October 16th

After school today I flopped on the sofa to watch a TV show about girls who turn into mermaids. Dad got back from work early and sat next to me. He got quite into the show and I even saw him wipe a tear away after the main mermaid got her tail stuck under a rock. Once the credits had rolled he got out a silver bag.

'A little something for my girl ready for Blarney Hall,' he said, handing it over.

I opened it straight away. It was a torch with a handle.

'A torch?' I asked.

'Even better, it's a wind-up torch so it doesn't need batteries. You just wind it like this,' he said, showing me how it worked. It was quite good and I figured it would be useful during the night at Blarney Hall.

winder

'Thanks, Dad,' I said.

'That is so not fair. Where's my torch?' said Joppin, looking up from the computer. Dad just ruffled his hair and made a quick escape into the kitchen.

Thursday, October 17th

Four days until we go to Blarney Hall! Everyone's talking about it. Mandy came in late today. In fact, she missed the times tables test. As she bundled in and sat down she showed us her arm and we realized the cast was gone! She was so excited she kept waving her arm around. Mr Winters thought she was putting her hand up and kept asking her what she wanted. She said she didn't know. Mr Winters started sighing and tutting.

Saturday, October 19th

I'm now fully packed for Blarney Hall. I have enough clothes for the three days. I also have the wind-up torch and £3 for buying sweets at the tuck shop. Soooooooooooooo excited! I wonder what it will be like.

Monday, October 21st

The rickety old bus rounded the corner and we saw Blarney Hall through the mist. It was a huge stone house surrounded by gardens. The road was lined with autumn trees, brown and orange leaves swirling off them as the wind shook the branches. I was so happy to get off the bus. I'd felt quite sick, and breathing in the cold autumn air settled my stomach. Dark clouds were rolling in, and we managed to run inside just as icy rain started falling.

We watched the rain from our dormitory window. Holly, Mandy, Sarah and I were sharing a room. We all sat on the top of one of the old metal bunk beds and shared some snacks. Suddenly, a rumble of thunder caused us all to drop our biscuits. We screamed and hid under a blanket.

After hearing the faint sound of Mr Winters' whistle, we went down to the dining hall. We all lined up to fill our plates with sweetcorn, burgers and chocolate-covered doughnuts. YUM!

As it was too wet to go outside Mr Winters proposed games in the main hall. We played dodge ball first and I was out straight away. Then we played a strange game where we had to balance beanbags on our heads. After that we did wheelbarrow races. I put my hands on the floor and Holly held my feet. It was hard not to laugh as I scuttled along on my hands, Holly laughing as she ran along behind me. We were quite fast though and we beat Peter and Jake in the wheelbarrow race final.

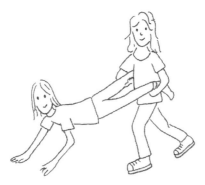

So here I am now in bed. I'm under the scratchy green blanket with my wind-up torch, diary and pen. It took quite a bit of winding to get enough light to write by but it seems to be working properly now. I think everyone else is asleep. I can hear snoring from at least two beds. I've got a feeling it's going to be a long night.

Tuesday, October 22nd

If I'd known at the beginning of the day what would have happened by the end of it, I would have stayed in bed. Oh, the embarrassment of it all!

The weather was much better today. There was even a little bit of sunshine squeezing through the clouds. 'As the weather is so good we will all be cooking hot dogs over the fire tonight,' said Mr Winters, as we all tucked into our breakfast. 'So keep an eye out for a good cooking stick to put your sausage on later.'

The plan for the day was to canoe for three miles then walk three miles back to Blarney Hall. Mr Winters made it very clear that we must only collect our cooking sticks once we were nearly back. 'I don't want people carrying sticks for three miles and I certainly don't want people canoeing with sticks,' he said.

We all nodded excitedly. Sitting around a campfire sounded like fun, although the last time I sat around a fire I got a very hot face. I decided to sit further away from the flames this time.

I wore jeans and my new purple waterproof coat. We set off on the walk down to the river. There were loads of leaves along the edge of the path and we kicked them about as we walked. Then I saw these two branches lying on the floor amongst the leaves.

'Look, Holly,' I said, 'these would be great for cooking the sausages.'

'No way, they're too big,' said Holly, as she kicked a small stone across the path.

'Exactly, we don't want to get hot faces by the fire do we? We can stand well back if we've got these,' I said, starting to pick them up.

'But we're not allowed to collect sticks until we're nearly back,' said Holly.

I picked them up and held them in the air. They were about the same length as my legs.

'Can we hide them and get them later?' asked Holly.

'Someone else will get them,' I said, sliding one branch down each leg of my jeans. As soon as I'd done it I realized that it wasn't my best idea as I couldn't bend my knees at all. I had to walk with very straight legs, which was very difficult. Holly started laughing. I tried to pull the sticks out but they were stuck.

'Come along, girls!' shouted Mr Winters, overtaking us. I ran along with my legs straight. I must have looked ridiculous. I ambled along in a strange manner until we got to the boats.

Holly had to help to slide my legs into the canoe. Once I was in it was OK. A straight leg problem in a canoe is doable.

The canoeing was hard work but quite fun. Holly kept splashing me with her paddle and my trousers ended up soaking wet from the waist to the knees. When we got to the end of the canoeing, I couldn't get out. Holly, Sarah and Mandy all had to pull me backwards and eventually I slid out, the sticks still stuck down my trousers. 'Come and sit on the benches for your sandwiches,' said Mr Winters. I managed to hobble over and sit on a bench with my legs straight out in front of me. Once we'd finished our sandwiches Mr Winters handed out large chocolate muffins. I was just devouring the last few crumbs when Mr Winters blew his whistle. 'Time for the hike,' he said, as he jumped up and started stretching.

Everyone moaned. I tried again to pull the sticks out of my jeans but the wetness had made them even more stuck than before. I had no choice. I was going to have to do the walk with straight legs.

I waddled along as the hike began. Holly and Sarah walked either side of me, linking my arms to help me along. This made it possible to do a sort of straight-leg glide for each step. Mr Winters gave me a strange look as he watched us go past.

'What are you doing?' he asked.

'Oh, um, stiff legs,' I said, stopping to rub my trousers. 'I'm sure they'll be alright in a minute.'

Luckily, Peter Potter fell into a huge puddle and Mr Winters jogged off to help him as we continued to waddle along. Later, Mr Winters came up to me

41

again. My legs were getting tired and my waddling was more extreme.

'Owwww, my legs,' I said, pretending they were hurting so he wouldn't be suspicious about the sticks.

'Are you sure you're OK?' he asked.

'Yes, yes, I'll manage,' I said.

I saw Mr Winters take out his phone and ring someone. The walk seemed to be going on forever. It felt so strange to be walking with sticks down my trousers. After a long time we turned a corner and saw Blarney Hall. Everyone cheered. Then we noticed an ambulance parked outside the entrance. We all started chatting about it, wondering what was going on.

As we got to the ambulance we noticed Mr Winters talking to the driver. Two paramedics ran up to me, grabbed me by the arms, and bundled me into the ambulance. I was so shocked I didn't complain. They laid me on a bed, my legs straight out in front of me.

'Best we check you out,' said a chubby lady paramedic in a neat green-and-white uniform. She got out various pieces of equipment then the ambulance set off with its siren on. The woman started taking my pulse, listening to my heart, and taking my blood pressure. I saw her glance at my wet trousers. She raised her eyebrows and made a note on a form.

Eventually, the ambulance stopped. The bed I was lying on was wheeled out of the vehicle and into the hospital. I could smell disinfectant as I was rushed along a white corridor. Suddenly, Mum was there, running along next to me. 'What's going on?' I asked her, trying to sit up.

'Oh, darling, we've been so worried. Mr Winters rang us and explained what happened.'

'What did happen?' I asked.

'Dr Motley is going to have a look at you. She's a specialist in serious leg problems. She's just come out of the operating theatre so she can examine you,' Mum said, a tear rolling down her cheek.

Dr Motley was standing in the corridor. She beckoned to the nurses to wheel me into a room. We went in, Mum too, and the trolley was stopped.

The doctor stood having a good look at me. I really wished my trousers were dry. 'Can you bend your legs?' she asked in a very serious voice.

'No, well yes, but not right now,' I said, blushing.

'Can you take your trousers off?' she asked, scratching her head.

I tried to lean down to pull them off but because of the sticks I couldn't bend my legs, which meant there was no way I could take them off.

'No, I can't,' I said, panic in my voice.

'We'll have to cut them off then,' she said. 'Then we can get you straight to X-ray. We have a team waiting in operating theatre two just in case.'

Two nurses who had been hovering about came up to me with scissors.

'She can't move her legs,' whispered one nurse to the other.

'Ohhh, serious,' said the other.

They cut my jeans, starting at the ankle and finishing at the waist. Just after they'd done the final snip, the two branches rolled out onto the trolley. I immediately bent my legs.

Everyone stared, speechless. Then Mum hugged me. I jumped off the trolley and bent my legs lots of times. It was such a relief to be able to move about as usual.

'Take her away,' said Dr Motley.

'What a time-waster,' said one of the nurses.

Mum and I left the room. I was embarrassed because I had no trousers on so Mum took me home to get changed then drove me back to Blarney Hall.

We got to Blarney Hall quite late. It was already dark and everything looked spooky in the moonlight. We walked around to the back gardens of the Hall and saw the bonfire. Lots of people were crouched around it cooking their hot dogs. I kissed Mum goodbye and walked over to Mr Winters. He gave me a spare stick and a sausage.

'So, what was up with your legs?' he asked. 'You seem a lot better now.'

'Oh, um, stiffiitus, something I may get now and then but I'm OK now,' I said, putting my sausage onto my stick. 'But, er, the doctor said no running for at least a year,' I said, as a clever afterthought.

'That's a shame as you were just getting into your running. But where one door closes another opens,' he said.

'Yes,' I said in a sad voice. I turned around and smiled.

RESULT!

Perhaps the day wasn't so bad after all.

I sat with the girls in the dark and we all ate sausages. We looked up at the stars.

'Funniest day ever,' said Sarah.

'It was hilarious,' said Mandy, holding her legs out straight.

'Best friends forever?' asked Holly. We all hooked our little fingers together and agreed.

Wednesday, October 23rd

Last night I stayed up late. I was under my cover with my wind-up torch doing detailed doodles of trees and hearts.

Today was the last day of the school trip. It was cold but dry and we went climbing. Mr Winters didn't want me to do it but I convinced him I was fine. He was amazed at my recovery and let me have a go. It was quite scary climbing up a cliff but I made it to the top. In the afternoon we all boarded the rickety old orange bus and left Blarney Hall. We sang songs all the way back to school.

It was so nice to get back home. I lay on the sofa under the orange blanket watching some TV. My brother Joppin came and sat right next to me. I think he'd missed me, although he'd never admit it.

Friday, October 25th

In art we had to draw pictures of our favourite memory from the Blarney Hall trip. All the pictures are going to be laminated and put up in the school hall.

Holly started drawing me walking along with stiff legs.

'How can me with stiff legs be your favourite memory of the holiday?' I asked.

'Well, it was the funniest thing ever,' said Holly.

'OK, but put yourself in too and don't make the stiffness too obvious,' I said.

She drew the two of us walking along. My legs looked very wide apart. I'm sure they weren't like that in real life.

Mandy drew the wheelbarrow race from the first night.

Sarah drew the maths quiz they did after the hike. I'd missed that as I was at the hospital.

I had to think for a long time. What was my favourite memory from the trip? I had a few ideas but there was one thing that was the highlight of the holiday for me – the time when everyone else was asleep and I was under my covers with the wind-up torch. I drew that. I wrote wind wind on the picture

47

because no one could see what I was doing under there.

Wednesday, October 30th

Holly's having a Halloween party tomorrow and my mum got me a terrible costume. It's not even a proper Halloween costume. It's a carrot suit which was originally made to advertise a vegetable shop. Apparently, the carrot outfit was so unsuccessful that the shop didn't sell any carrots for a month after it was used. In the end someone gave it to Mum to sell in her eBay shop.

'It's not very Halloweenish,' I said to her.

'Well, it's all we've got, although I suppose you could be a ghost and wear Dad's white pyjamas, you know, the ones with the yellow stains,' she said.

I decided to be a carrot.

To make the costume scary, I'm going to cover it in fake worms. I found this old stringy mop behind the fridge and cut off all the strings to drape over the top of the carrot.

Thursday, October 31st
HALLOWEEN

So there I was, a carrot with stringy worm hair waddling down the street to Holly's house. It was qute hard to walk, as the carrot leg holes were too far apart. Luckily, I'd had some practice of this style of walking at Blarney Hall.

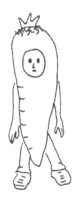

'What on earth are you?' asked Holly, as she opened the door. Holly was a very glamorous witch with striped tights and a glitter wig. 'Mandy, Sarah, come and take a look at this!' she shouted.

They all ran to the door and looked at me. Mandy was dressed as a black cat and Sarah as a silk pumpkin.

'I know, I know, Mum got it for me,' I said, bundling into the house. Everyone except me sat down. I found out that I couldn't sit down. The carrot costume was kind of solid so I had to balance on the tip.

'Is it a real Halloween costume?' asked Holly's mum, as she offered me an eyeball cake.

'No, but I've made it scary by adding these worms,' I said, pointing to the stringy bits of mop on the top.

'Oh yes, scary worms, very good,' she said, rushing out of the room to get some blood juice.

When I told Holly that it was hard to walk in the costume, she said she had a brilliant idea. She got a skateboard out of the garage and tied some string to it.

'Don't worry, I'll pull the carrot along,' she said, beaming.

'Thanks, Holly,' I said.

After a few games we went out to do the trick or treating. I was pulled along on the skateboard behind Holly. We passed groups of kids dressed up as ghosts, mummies and witches. They all laughed when they saw us.

'Skateboarding carrot!' they shouted.

We knocked on the door of a house, and an old lady opened it.

'Oh, you look lovely,' she said as she examined our costumes. She then looked at my head, 'Oh dear, there's some rubbish on you,' she said, grabbing my mop worms. 'I'll pop these in the bin,' she added, rushing off with them! When she returned, she offered us each a lolly.

I'd become a wormless carrot with no scary attributes. I wondered how I could look Halloweenish now. I decided to pull a fierce face at the next house.

We knocked on the next door. 'Oh dear,' said the man, looking at my twisted face. 'You can use my toilet if you need to.'

'Um, I'm fine,' I said. I can't believe my scariest face makes it look like I need the toilet. I decided to be a plain old carrot.

We got loads of sweets and started eating them straight away. Overall it was a very successful Halloween, although it was lovely to take my costume off and get into bed at the end of the night.

Monday, November 4th

A strange thing happened as I arrived at school this morning. I slung my bag over my shoulder and ran into the school playground to look for Holly. As I made my way through the crowds of kids I noticed that people were pointing at me and mumbling as I went past.

I checked my trousers – no toilet paper was hanging out. I checked my clothes – no Weetabix was spilt down my front. I saw Holly and rushed over.

'Do I look normal?' I asked.

She looked at me for a while. 'Hmmmm, well, same as usual,' she said, checking my front and back.

'So why is everyone looking at me?' I asked.

'Oh, that. I know', she said, 'It's that Blarney Hall drawing you did. It's been up in the hall since Friday. Someone said it was funny, but I'm not sure why.'

'Oh?' I couldn't figure out what the big deal was. 'It's just me with my wind-up torch in bed,' I said.

The bell rang and we all ran into school. I was very confused. How could a drawing of me under my duvet cause so much interest? In the morning I pretended I needed the toilet then sneaked into the hall to see the drawing, in case someone had changed it. It looked just the same as when I'd done it.

At playtime Jake came up to me holding his nose.

'The best part of your school trip was passing wind in bed,' he said, laughing.

I cringed as I realised I'd written the word 'wind' (wind up torch) on my picture, but it looked like I'd written 'wind' (as in passing wind).

'Bu-bu-bu-but I was winding up my torch,' I said in a panic.

'Never heard it called that before,' said Jake, wafting his hand in front of his nose.

I went up to as many people as I could.

'There's been a misunderstanding. I was winding my torch,' I said desperately. This just made things worse as everyone started talking about it even more. At least seven people held their noses when they came near me. There was nothing I could do. I just had to put up with it.

Friday, November 8th

It's been a tough week but pretending I don't care seems to have been the best strategy. Fewer people are going on about the wind/wind thing now. Luckily, Peter did a wee in the playground yesterday and that seems to be the new funny story.

GO WOODLICE

We got our team points for our buddy books today. The little kids rated our books: one for poor, two for OK and three for good. All the points were put on the Royalty, Mammals or Woodlice posters. I was overjoyed as I got a three. I decided to thank Riley at buddy time on Monday.

The Woodlice team now has fifty points, Royalty has forty-seven, and Mammals has thirty-six!

Yippee! I feel a trip to The Big Apple (aka New York) coming my way. Could this be the big win?

Monday, November 11th
BUDDY DAY

I couldn't find my winter hat this morning so Dad made me wear his balaclava. This is like a black hat that covers my whole head with a hole for the eyes. It's a bit embarrassing to wear but it's so cold I'm wearing it anyway.

At buddy time I scanned the playground for my little buddy. I saw him in the corner and I was pleased to see he wasn't on his own. He was with another little boy. I think it was the boy who was talking to him about the bogeyman book the other week.

I decided to give them a treat. I sneaked up behind them wearing my balaclava and did a bogeyman impression, my arms flailing in the wind.

' Boooooogggggeymaaaan wiiiilllll geeetttt youuuuu!' I yelled.

Riley and his friend spun round, their mouths and eyes wide open. They ran off screaming to the other end of the playground.

Wednesday, November 13th

Holly, Sarah and I are going to Mandy's for tea on Saturday. She's got some new roller skates and she's desperate to show them off.

'Roller skating is easy,' she said today. 'I can even go backwards.'

I quite like going to Mandy's house. She's got so much stuff. She's got computer game systems, a TV, a laptop, an iPad and a Furby in her glamorous gold-and-cream bedroom.

I on the other hand have got very little. I'm not allowed anything electrical in my room. I do have a notebook and a bookshelf. I would love my own TV. We only have one main TV in the lounge and I have to share it with Mum, Dad and Joppin. This is most annoying because Joppin likes silly cartoons and Mum has an obsession with the news. This means it's quite rare for me to watch anything I like. I do have a favourite programme – it's called *Bedroom Makeover*. Luckily, it's one of the few non-cartoon programmes that Joppin likes so I do get to see it now and then.

I would LOVE a bedroom makeover. In fact, I've written four times to ask if I can go on the show but they never reply. My room is pretty awful. The walls are covered in garish wallpaper with huge pink cartoon flowers. I can't bear to look at it and I often have to sit in the dark just to get away from it. Mum got the wallpaper for nothing when I was a baby. The shopkeeper couldn't sell it so he gave it to her just to get rid of it. Whenever I say how awful it is, she reminds me that it would have cost £100 a roll if she'd had to pay for it. Apparently, this means that I must never complain about it.

Saturday, November 16th
MANDY'S HOUSE

There was light snow in the air as Dad and I drew up outside Mandy's big stone house. I waved goodbye to him and rushed in to see if the others were already there. Holly opened the door.

'Hooray, you're here!' she said, bustling me in. Mandy had the roller skates on and she was whizzing up and down the varnished wooden floor of the hall, her shiny blond hair swishing behind her. Sarah was running along next to her.

We all had a go with the roller skates. My feet are on the small side so they were massive on me. I think this is why I was so bad. I wavered about a bit then fell flat on my back, looking up at a crystal chandelier. Holly was much better than me. She managed to skate right up the hall and do a spin turn then skate back again.

After quite a long time in the hall we all went up to Mandy's bedroom. It was very beautiful with cream walls, a cream-and-gold duvet cover, and a gold desk and office chair. There was a TV on the wall and a row of white furry beanbags all along one side of the room.

Mandy put on the delicate fairy lights, which hung all around the ceiling, and we all sat on the beanbags. I rested my cheek against the soft fabric and felt like a baby polar bear nestling into a big polar bear.

'What would be really great would be a roller-skating party,' said Mandy, doing a strange thumbs up movement.

'My birthday's soon so I could do it,' said Holly, spinning round so she was upside down on her beanbag with her feet against the wall.

'We could all get roller skates for Christmas ready for the party,' added Sarah excitedly.

'Yep. My birthday is February the 3rd. I wonder if I could hire St Margaret's Church Hall,' said Holly.

It was all decided – Holly would be having a roller-skating disco party. It sounds good but I'm very worried as my parents are not very reliable when it comes to Christmas presents. They prefer to give me things they've made themselves and they hate buying anything new. Dad says it's a waste of money to buy things. But perhaps with enough begging they'll change their minds.

We had tea at Mandy's – pizza and dough balls with cucumber sticks and chocolate cake for pudding. YUM!! It was funny because Mandy's dad dressed up as a butler and brought everything through on a silver tray.

Sunday, November 17th

'Dad,' I said this morning, as I tucked into my cornflakes, 'I'd love some roller skates for Christmas.' I held my breath while he looked into the air, thinking.

'OK, I think it's possible,' he said.

'YIPPPPPEEEEE!' I can't wait for Christmas now. This may be the first year that I get a real, shop-bought present rather than something dodgy out of Dad's workshop.

It's only five-and-a-bit weeks until Christmas!!!! Then it will be about five weeks between Christmas and Holly's birthday. This is good, as I will have ages to practise and get good at skating. I may even learn a routine to do at the disco. Perhaps I could even learn to go backwards. Soooooo excited!

This afternoon I wrote plans for my roller-skating routine and drew myself doing it.

Forwards for four metres.
Spin round one-and-a-half times.

Backwards for three metres.
Spin round one-and-a-half times.
Do a fancy zigzag-style move.
Mega spin.
Bow.

I had a look on YouTube for ideas and found some amazing skaters on there. I'm going to practise in my mind until I get the skates. I remember Grandma telling me that imagined practising is almost as good as real practising. Apparently, there are experiments to prove this.

Monday, November 18th
BUDDY DAY

I decided to be very normal during the buddy session today.

'Hi, Riley,' I said, wandering up to him.

'Hi,' he said in a tiny voice before running off. Result! I got a word out of him. Things are looking good. He didn't appear to want to have a longer chat so I joined Holly and Mary. We played follow the leader. When it was my turn to be the leader, I was about to do my zombie walk when I noticed Riley watching from behind a tree. I decided to do a sensible grown-up walk instead.

Thursday, November 21st
PERIL

Something very strange happened today. We all went into our classroom as usual this morning but Mr Winters was nowhere to be seen. We were sitting around chatting when we heard the door creak open. Then someone dressed up as a monster ran into the room. Lots of people screamed but we all laughed when the monster started blowing his whistle. The monster wrote 'PERIL' on the whiteboard in large letters.

'What is seven times seven?' the monster growled.

'Forty-nine,' we all sang back at him.

He took his costume off. Yes, it was Mr Winters looking a bit bedraggled with messy hair.

'OK,' he said, 'who can tell me what peril is?'

No one said anything.

'No? I will tell you. It is where you are faced with danger or fear. Like you were when I came in dressed as Mosby monster. You experienced peril. You felt that you were in danger.'

Everyone watched him eagerly, wondering what it was all about.

'My hypothesis is,' he continued, 'that we learn better when we are in peril, so I shall be doing various scary activities with you to help you with your learning.'

There was a buzz of excitement around the room. Jake started shouting 'boo' at people.

'Get out, Jake,' said Mr Winters. 'I provide the peril not you.'

Jake shuffled out of the room and stood outside the door. He knows where to stand because he's sent out most days. After five minutes Mr Winters called him back in again.

After lunch we had our first peril lesson. We all went into the playground where we were blindfolded. We then had to walk along a plank of wood while reciting the eight times table. It was quite scary trying to stay on the plank and I only managed to get to three times eight. I'm not sure about this peril theory.

Saturday, November 23rd
Only four-and-a-half weeks until Christmas. I watched some more roller-skating films on YouTube and did some mind practice. I'm getting quite good at it. I did at least twenty spins in my head. I just hope I'm as good when I get the roller skates for real.

Thursday, November 28th
We had another peril lesson today. We had to put one hand in a bowl of iced water while writing out our spellings with the other hand. It didn't help me

to remember my spellings – in fact, it put me off. I put my dry hand up.

'I can't concentrate, Mr Winters,' I said.

Mr Winters thought for a minute. 'Ahaaaaa,' he said, 'but just think, when you do your spellings without your hand in icy water, you will be so relieved you will be able to concentrate better.' He looked smug as he made a note in his notebook. I noticed there was a sticker on the front of his book with the word 'peril' on it.

Saturday, November 30th

Not long until Christmas now. I did ten minutes of practising in my mind today. I'm going to be so good when I practise for real.

Sunday, December 1st

I asked Mum if we could put the Christmas tree up today. She said, 'No, we have to wait one more week.'

We have the same spindly Christmas tree every year. There's a box of decorations to go with it, all home-made by Joppin and me when we were toddlers. (They don't look that good.) Mum says she's going to get some pine cones for us to decorate this year so it could look a bit better than normal. Anyway, despite the tree being ropey I'm keen to get it out as I love it when the house feels all Christmassy.

There's one problem in our house at Christmas though. It's Joppin's birthday on Christmas Eve. Mum says it's not fair to have all the Christmas decorations up on Joppin's birthday, so we have to take everything down and put all the presents in the garage for the day. No one is allowed to mention Christmas even though it's the very next day.

Monday, December 2nd

BUDDY DAY

Today was buddy day. Because it was wet playtime we all had to go into the reception classroom for buddy time.

'Just play with your buddy,' said Mrs Rizla, smiling.

Everyone rushed up to their buddy. I looked for Riley. I couldn't see him anywhere but another boy pointed to the corner of the room. I looked and found him crouched on the floor behind a bin. I saw one big brown eye peer up at me.

'Shall we play a game?' I asked, leaning over the bin.

'No, thank you,' he said, rolling into a tiny ball on the floor.

I saw Mr Winters come into the room. Thinking there may be Woodlice points on offer for playing nicely with your buddy I had to act fast. I crouched down next to Riley. 'Great idea for a game,' I said loudly, as I crawled into the space next to him, both of us squashed behind the bin with me rolled into a ball too. Riley looked at me, then rushed out of his hiding spot and ran over to the little boy he'd been playing with last week.

Mrs Rizla came over to me as I clambered out of the small space.

'Maggie, good work! I've been trying to get him out of there all morning,' she said.

Mr Winters came over too, nodding approvingly. 'A point for Woodlice,' he said. 'Well done, Maggie!'

YIPPEE!

Wednesday, December 4th

Today we found out about the school Christmas concert. Our class will be playing Jingle Bells on the recorder. After that we'll all dress up as Christmas presents to sing and dance under a Christmas tree.

We were each given a recorder to borrow until after the concert. We learnt recorder a few years ago in class three but most people had forgotten how to play. It sounded terrible when we did that first practice. I could see that Mr Winters was trying not to wince as he listened.

We all got to take our recorders home to practise before the next rehearsal on Friday.

Friday, December 6th

We had recorder again today – Jingle Bells sounded better. You could just about tell what song it was. Sarah's been learning the recorder for eight years so she could play it brilliantly. She was so good that Mr Winters said she could play the first verse on her own and then everyone else could join in for the chorus. I saw Sarah glow with pride.

Sunday, December 8th

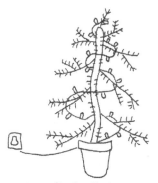

Mum let us put our little Christmas tree up today. I managed to persuade her to leave the toddler decorations and just put the multi-coloured lights on it. It looks nice but it does need more decorations. I wish we could have shiny glass baubles, tiny hanging Santa models or glittery stars like other people.

'Do you need help choosing the roller skates?' I asked Dad, as we put the toddler decorations back in the box.

'No, I'm already onto it,' he said, smiling.

YEEEEEEESSSSS! This means that it's probably going to happen. I'm probably going to get a proper Christmas present this year. My very own roller skates.

WHOOOOOOPPPPPEEEEEEE!

Monday, December 9th

We had more recorder practice today. It's definitely sounding better. When Sarah starts playing on her own, it sounds amazing, but when everyone joins in, it sounds a bit random.

We also started making our Christmas present costumes for the Christmas tree dance. This involved gluing wrapping paper onto big boxes. I'm very glad that everyone has the same part this year. I usually get the very worst part in the play so this is quite a rare treat for me.

BUDDY TIME

I didn't even try to talk to Riley today but he glanced at me as he went in at the end of playtime.

Tuesday, December 10th

We finished off our Christmas present outfits for the concert. Everyone looks so funny. After I'd been wearing my box for a while I forgot I was inside a box and went to sit down. As I lowered myself towards the chair I fell flat on my back. Everyone was in hysterics as I lay there, unable to get up.

Mr Winters ran into the room. 'Maggie, get up this instant!' he shouted.

I thought this was particularly mean as I'd obviously fallen accidentally and was clearly unable to get up. Mrs Rizla ran into the room. 'It's not funny,' she said, crossing her arms and frowning. In the end Sarah and Mandy helped me up and we went into the hall for our practice. There's going to be a big tree on the stage and the 'presents' will dance around under it while singing:

'We are dancing presents
underneath a tree.
Lots of dancing presents
For you and for me.'

Then we all have to jump up and down while singing:

'We are jumping presents
underneath a tree.
Lots of jumping presents
For you and for me.'

The song carries on like this with us spinning, jogging and then stamping.

It felt a little bit babyish but Mrs Rizla assured us that it looked brilliant and it was kind of fun, especially the stamping.

Wednesday, December 11th

I've found out that we're having a class Christmas party next Wednesday! Everyone has to take something in and I'm taking in chocolate buns. I'll have to have a word with Mum to see if I can bake them over the weekend. I want Holly to come round and bake with me – that would be so much fun.

Friday, December 13th

Good news! I asked Mum if Holly could come over on Sunday and she said yes.

I asked if Holly and I could bake buns for the party and she said yes to that too!

It's all getting quite Christmassy at school now. We made Christmas cards today. We drew Christmas pictures on the computer then printed them out to glue onto card.

We also practised the recorder. I sounded pretty good – in fact, Mrs Rizla said that I was the second best after Sarah. Sarah's brilliant though. When she plays, she sounds so much better than anyone else. It's kind of weird.

Saturday, December 14th

After breakfast, Mum emptied out a bag of pine cones out onto the table. Their foresty smell filled the air and reminded me of our last camping trip. After putting newspapers down she got out PVA glue, different coloured pots of glitter, and pipe cleaners.

We poured glue over the pine cones then sprinkled the glitter on and finished off by winding pipe cleaners round to make loops to hang them on the tree. They're currently drying on the windowsill. They're going to make the tree look much better. I want it to look nice for when Holly comes round tomorrow.

<u>Sunday, December 15th</u>
HOLLY DAY

I saved one of the multi-coloured glitter pine cones for Holly. I wrapped it in special orange tissue paper and put it in a gift bag.

Holly arrived just after lunch. Mum had got all the cake-making things ready and gone outside to rake leaves with Joppin. Holly and I began the important work of bun making.

It was a messy business with lots of flour everywhere. We even got dough on our faces when we licked the bowl. It was all incredibly disorganized with ingredients all over the place.

'And into the oven they go,' said Holly.

We looked at them through the glass oven door. All that effort put into little bun cases. I couldn't wait for them to be ready.

'Let's go and wait in the lounge. I want to show you our tree,' I said, pulling Holly through.

'Great tree but what are those?' Holly pointed at the glitter pine cones on the windowsill.

'Sparkle cones for the tree. What do you think?'

'Oh, very multi-coloured,' she said, flopping down onto the sofa. 'We've just got gold baubles. Mum says just one colour looks best.'

I looked at the multi-coloured lights and the multi-coloured cones. I decided to keep quiet about the fact that I'd made them. I also decided not to give Holly the one I'd made for her. I think it'll look good hanging on my bedroom door instead.

Soon the smell of delicious buns filled the air. We rushed through to the kitchen and checked through the glass door. They looked perfect. We ate one each as the others cooled then decorated them with ready-made icing and small silver balls.

After the bun making we went up to my room.

'I can't wait for my roller-skating party,' said Holly.

'I know. I asked my Dad for skates for Christmas and he actually said yes.'

'I'm getting some amazing pink-and-white ones,' said Holly.

Wednesday, December 18th
SCHOOL CHRISTMAS PARTY

The table was full of crisps, sandwiches and cakes. My buns were on a tray in the middle and they looked pretty good. We'd arranged the silver balls in all different patterns and they sparkled under the moving lights.

Music played and some of the boys were breakdancing. The girls and I stood in a corner.

'I'm having disco lights at my roller-skating party,' said Holly.

'Get a ramp,' added Mandy. 'We can do jumps.' Everyone agreed that this was a brilliant idea.

Mr Winters started organizing games. We played tig, musical statues and then wheelbarrow races. I was Holly's partner in the wheelbarrow race and we came second.

Thursday, December 19th

Tomorrow night is the school Christmas concert for the parents. We spent most of this morning practising the recorder then we had a dress rehearsal of the Christmas present dance. I think we're having one last practice tomorrow with the whole school. Jingle Bells sounds quite good now. I was quite pleased because Mrs. Rizla came up to me at the end of the practice and said that my recorder playing was sounding beautiful.

Friday, December 20th
LAST DAY OF TERM

In the morning we had one big practice ready for tonight. We also got to see what all the other classes are doing. Joppin is going to be a marble in a marble run dance.

All the seats are set up in the hall and the teachers are rushing about tidying up displays and trying to make the school look more organized.

TEAM CUP

In the afternoon Mr Winters announced which class team had won the cup for the most points this term. Woodlice won!

'This just goes to show that it doesn't matter which group you are in. It makes no difference to your chances of winning,' he said.

If team Woodlice is still in the lead at the end of the school year, in September, we'll win the trip to The Big Apple. We're going to have to work hard to keep Woodlice in the lead. After school Quentin came up to me and patted me on the back.

'Nice work, Woodlouse,' he said. Mandy sneered at him and said that it didn't matter who won as it's joining in that's important. I went home delighted that team Woodlice was doing so well.

I'm going back to school at seven p.m. for the concert.

Friday, December 20th

LATER – CONCERT NEWS

I met up with Holly and Mandy in the playground before the concert. Mum and Dad went into the hall.

'Where's your recorder?' asked Mandy, waving hers around. I froze. I knew straight away that I'd forgotten it. We all stood in shocked silence.

'Just hide at the back,' said Holly. 'No one will notice.'

I looked up at the sky hoping for inspiration. Then I saw the big tree at the end of the playground and had a brilliant idea. I sprinted towards it as fast as I could and scrabbled around in the leaves at the foot of the tree. I found a stick, broke a piece off, and bundled it up my sleeve. I heard a familiar whistle and ran in with everyone else.

Once I was sitting down I got my stick out under the table and drew some black dots on it to look like holes. It didn't look that much like a recorder but I figured that as I stood at the back no one would notice. All I needed to do was hold it to my lips while hiding behind everyone else.

'You are on in two minutes,' said Mr Winters, 'but where's Sarah?'

Everyone looked around. Sarah was nowhere to be seen. Mrs Rizla ran in looking all flustered.

'All the parents are in,' said Mrs Rizla, 'a TV crew are here too. They're covering our show for the news.'

Mr Winters went up to her. 'Sarah's not here,' he said in a very serious voice.

Mrs Rizla went bright red. 'Line up, everyone,' she said. I took my position at the back of the line, hiding my recorder stick behind my back. 'Now, Maggie, you are going to have to take Sarah's place and do the solo,' she said, as she pulled me to the front. I was bundled onto the stage with the rest of the children.

I gripped my stick, wondering what to do. Mum waved at me. I did a nervous smile. The room was silent and a spotlight lit me up. Everyone waited for me to play.

I held the stick up to my lips. I don't think anyone noticed at first. It was when I began to make a noise like a recorder that the laughter started. I began singing 'dee, dee, dee' to the tune of Jingle Bells and people looked astonished. The TV camera was focussed on me. I was shaking but I carried on for the whole first verse. I was very relieved when everyone else joined in. At the end I ran off. Mrs Rizla ran after me.

'What on earth were you doing?' she asked.

'I, I forgot my recorder,' I said.

'We'll be the laughing stock of the country,' she said, putting her head in her hands.

Everyone started talking about how funny it was.

'I think it sounded OK,' said Holly.

We all had to change into the Christmas present outfits and wait until it was time for 'We are dancing presents'. I decided to keep a low profile and dance at the back.

We went on and did our dancing, jumping and stamping. Just as we were about to run off Jack accidentally knocked me over. Everyone else left the stage but I was left lying on my back. My arms and legs were wriggling as I attempted to get up. The audience were in hysterics. Mr Winters and Mrs Rizla ran on and carried me off. Once back in the classroom I got changed into my normal clothes as quickly as possible.

'What are you doing, Maggie, trying to make us look like fools?' asked Mrs Rizla. I sat in silence.

Saturday, December 21st
ON THE NEWS

Amazing news, I'm famous (sort of). On the local news there was a bit about the school play. They showed two clips – one of me pretending to play the stick recorder and one of me in my Christmas present outfit being carried off the stage. They said it was a comedy masterpiece. I'm just glad that it's now the school holidays so I don't have to face Mrs Rizla and Mr Winters for two weeks.

Sunday, December 22nd
Four days until Christmas (including today).

Monday, December 23rd
Three days until I'm the owner of roller skates!

Tuesday, December 24th
JOPPIN'S BIRTHDAY
We had to put the tree away and put all the presents in the garage. Joppin got all his birthday presents. He got a home-made bowling set made of old bottles and a home-made balance board made out of a piece of wood with a ball stuck on underneath. I got him a SpongeBob annual as I know how disappointing it is if all your presents are hand-made. The balance board was quite fun though.

Wednesday, December 25th
CHRISTMAS DAY
No, no, no, no, no!
I should've known it was too good to be true. I woke up this morning so excited about the new roller skates. I had visions of an afternoon skating along the

pavement near my house, showing the neighbours my lovely new skates.

The time came to open the presents. I was handed a large shoebox-shaped gift. It was the right size and the right weight. Mum and Dad held hands as I opened it. Dad had a huge grin on his face. I undid the woollen bow and then unwrapped the potato-printed wrapping paper to reveal a large shoebox inside. I frisbeed the lid across the floor and peered in.

There inside the box was a pair of old black walking boots with Joppin's old buggy wheels screwed onto them. The wheels looked huge and strange. Overall they looked very wrong.

I stared at them, wondering if anyone would jump up and say 'It's a joke! Here are your real skates!' No one did.

'Well, are you going to try them on, love?' asked Mum.

'You'll never believe this but I made them myself,' said Dad, as he rushed over and pulled them out of the box.

There they stood on the carpet. Hideous scruffy boots with massive wheels. Once they were on I found out they were wobbly and impossible to control.

'It's lucky I found those buggy wheels. My other thought was cotton reels,' Dad said, giving me a push.

'Careful,' I said, as I fell forward onto the sofa.

'You're all sorted for your skating party now, love,' said Dad.

'Yes, thank you,' I said.

We opened the rest of the presents – an assortment of odd home-made gifts. Joppin got me one proper present though – a cushion in the shape of a cupcake, which I like.

I also had a present from Holly that I'd promised to save until Christmas day. It was a cat's cradle kit. This consists of a long string tied into a loop and a booklet. You hook the string around different fingers to make different shapes.

'I remember that from my school days,' said Mum, having a go. We spent quite a few hours practising the basic shapes.

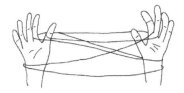

Sunday, December 29th

I had a nightmare about the roller boots last night. I dreamt I was rolling down a hill and couldn't stop. People were pointing and shouting as I wobbled past.

I did try them outside yesterday though. I waited until it was really dark and no one was about. Then with the help of Mum's shoulder, I went along for about five metres.

'You're going to be great by the time of the party, darling,' said Mum.

I remained quiet. I can't wear them to the party but I can't tell Mum that.

Monday, January 6th

I met up with the girls before school. We huddled in a corner of the playground. Holly had got each of us a cat's cradle kit and we'd brought them in. Quite a few people came over to see what was going on. I think it could become a craze.

'I got brilliant roller skates for Christmas. They are pink,' said Holly, as she stretched the loops out over her fingers.

'Me too,' said Sarah. 'White ones with flashing wheels.' They looked at me.

'Me three,' I said. I had to change the subject. 'Um, who can make "the basket of diamonds" the quickest?' I asked. We all started moving our string about like mad.

'Me!' shouted Mandy, holding hers up.

We got to visit our buddies at playtime. Riley ignored me so I helped Holly show Mary how to do cat's cradle.

At the end of school Mr Winters asked me to stay back for a chat. I waited in the empty classroom, moving my weight from one leg to the other. Mr Winters walked in.

'We need to have a chat about your behaviour.' He perched on the edge of his desk. 'Your behaviour during the concert was appalling. Any more trouble and I'll have to get your parents in. Do you understand?'

'But...'

'Do you understand?'

'Yes, sir.'

Wednesday, January 8th

Today we were given a chance to earn points for our teams. Woodlice is in the lead but we need to keep the points total up so I concentrated hard.

'This task is all about teamwork. You will work together to make towers out of dried spaghetti and marshmallows,' said Mr Winters.

Everyone started cheering.

'But you must NOT eat anything,' he added.

Royalty was given the carpet area next to the window, Mammals was in the reading corner, and Woodlice was in the corridor by the toilets. We all started sticking spaghetti onto the marshmallows in a random way. Quentin became very bossy and started drawing plans. All the other Woodlice seemed to go along with his ideas so I did too.

I sneaked a couple of marshmallows into my mouth when no one was looking. Mr Winters came over.

'Looking good, Woodlice. Tell me what you did first, Maggie?' he said.

I looked at him, my mouth full of marshmallows. I shrugged.

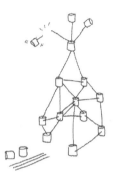

'Pardon, Maggie? I didn't quite hear that,' he said.

'The base,' I said through the marshmallow mush in my mouth. Mr Winters stared at me and then asked Quentin the same question. Quentin started talking all about physics. Mr Winters nodded, looking very impressed.

At the end of the day the task results were announced and guess what? Woodlice won. We got five team points. Waaaaaahooooooo!

Thursday, January 9th

Good news! We're going on a school trip next week. On Friday the 17th of January, in one week and one day, we're going to the new handwriting museum in town. Everyone was mumbling with excitement. Even though it's only a museum, it's still good to get out of school and go on a coach.

'I have a friend at the museum and this class has been given an amazing opportunity,' Mr Winters said. He then took out his whistle and blew it even though everyone was sitting quietly. 'When we are there, each child will do his or her neatest writing on a square tile.' He paused. I saw him look at his whistle but he decided not to blow it. 'Once fired, the tiles will be placed around the door or the museum so your handwriting samples will become part of the building.'

Everyone started talking at once. Mr Winters blew his whistle and silence fell across the room.

'What do we write about, sir?' asked Quentin.

'Something about writing, perhaps the history of writing or what it's for, something interesting.'

'How long will the tiles be up for?' asked Sarah.

'Forever. Future generations will see your work so make sure it is the best you can do,' he said.

Once home I practised my handwriting. It's quite neat although I do sometimes a draw circle over my 'i'. I'm always getting told off for it so I practised writing 'i' with a neat little dot over it.

Friday, January 10th

Mr Winters says he's going to give five team points for the five best handwriting samples next week. Hmmmm, better get practising as we can't afford to become complacent just because we're in the lead.

Our homework is to write a short piece about writing. This is actually going to be the message we'll write out on our tiles so it has to be good.

After school the girls and I all met up for a little cat's cradle practice. I can now do 'the clock' and 'the manger.'

Saturday, January 11th

Today I did my homework. I wrote: 'I like writing. In fact, I keep a diary. I write about lots of interesting things that happen to me.'

Monday, January 13th

We had to read our homework out. I read mine with great confidence. Mr Winters said, 'Hmmmm. OK, I guess.'

Quentin read his out. It was all about the Latin origins of certain words. Sarah's was about the importance of written communication in history.

Mandy's was about the use of different pens from feather quills to pink glitter gel pens. Holly's was about writing letters and all the different sorts of letters there could be.

I wondered if mine was a bit simple. Still, no one has mentioned a diary so at least it was different.

Tuesday, January 14th

We practised writing our homework pieces out for most of the morning. I did mine mega neat and added a nice loop for the 'y' and the 'g'. It's going to look really good when I write it on the tile.

After lunch we had maths. We'd been doing cat's cradle all lunchtime and we wanted to carry on practising, so we'd sneaked our string into the classroom and we continued making shapes under the tables. Unfortunately, Mr Winters saw us.

'That's it,' he said. 'Cat's cradle is banned.'

Even worse, he took all the cat's cradle kits and locked them in a cupboard.

When I got home, I told Mum I'd lost my string. She was sympathetic and she quickly made me a new loop out of pale pink wool.

Wednesday, January 15th

Holly handed out her birthday party invitations today. It's going to be on Saturday, the 1st of

February. She's hired St Margaret's Church Hall for the roller-skating party. After the skating bit we're all going back to her house for a party tea and then the three of us will stay for a sleepover. At the bottom of the invitation written in shiny pink pen were the words 'Don't forget your skates'. Eeeeeeeeeeek!

Once they'd read the invitations Mandy and Sarah grabbed each other's hands and started jumping up and down. I jumped up and down very slightly so I looked excited. In reality I was worried, very worried.

Thursday, January 16th

The school trip to the handwriting museum is tomorrow. I've decided to sneak my woollen loop onto the bus so I can practise cat's cradle on the way. If I sit quite far away from Mr Winters, it should be fine.

I'm still worried about the roller skates. I was up most of last night thinking about it. I've got three possible plans at the moment. Firstly, I could paint the skates white-and-pink so they look more like proper skates, secondly, I could put mirrors on them so they reflect other people's skates and it looks like I'm wearing their skates (hmmm), and thirdly, I could wear large trousers that cover up most of the skates.

I'll investigate these at the weekend.

Friday, January 17th
SCHOOL TRIP TO THE HANDWRITING MUSEUM

'You can't play with that on the bus,' whispered Sarah, as I got my pink woollen loop out and hooked it round my fingers.

'It's OK. Mr Winters is miles away.'

The bus set off for the handwriting museum. Some people at the back started singing.

'Shut up!' shouted the grumpy bus driver. We sat quietly for the rest of the journey.

I was in the middle of doing a very complicated cat's cradle move called 'the dog and his kennel' when Mr Winters started walking up the aisle of the coach towards me. In a panic I tried to get the pink wool off my fingers, but the more I struggled, the more tangled up it got. The wool had turned into a big knot. I managed to get my left hand out of the knot but my right hand was entangled tightly in the wool. There was nothing I could do – my hand was caught, the fingers tied together tightly. I jammed my tied hand into my pocket just before Mr Winters got to us. Phew!

'Is everyone behaving back here?' he asked.

We all nodded.

Soon we pulled up outside a modern building with 'Handwriting Museum' written in silver letters above the door. There was a black space around the door where we guessed the tiles would be going.

I kept my tied-up hand in my pocket as we got off the bus and went into the building. A woman with bright pink hair met us in the reception. 'OK, children, follow me to see the handwriting of famous people,' she said, waving a pink pointing stick in the air. We looked at framed pieces of paper with different handwriting on them.

'This is by Charles Dickens,' she said, pointing at some brownish paper, 'and this was written by the Queen,' she added, pointing to writing on special headed paper.

After looking at the samples for what felt like a long time we went into the activity room. I tried to separate my fingers in my pocket but they were still firmly tied up. I was beginning to worry that it might affect my handwriting as it was the fingers of my writing hand.

We all sat down with our square tiles. Everyone started copying out their pieces of writing using special purply-black pens. I slipped my mangled hand, still entwined with wool, from my pocket. Because the wool was light pink it wasn't too obvious to Mr Winters, who was sitting at the other side of the room.

I slid my pen into the wool and tried to write. I had to move my whole hand in order to make the pen move and it took me ages just to do one word. The writing looked terrible, like a two-year-old had done it. It was massive and wobbly. I could only fit the words 'I like writing' on the tile.

Holly finished her super-neat writing and looked over. She stared at mine.

'You can't hand that in,' she said. 'Let me do it for you.'

'I'm collecting them in now,' said Mrs Moritz, as she started skipping about the room. As she collected mine in she smiled and patted me on the head.

We had a toilet break next. I ran my woolly hand under the tap and, after adding lots of soap, managed to pull the wool off. I put it in one of the bathroom bins.

After we'd eaten our packed lunches we went back into the activity room.

'Good news, children. Your tiles are ready to go into the kiln,' said Mrs Moritz. 'This will make the writing permanent.'

All the tiles were spread out all across a table.

'They'll be going up on the wall outside tomorrow,' said Mrs Moritz.

Mr Winters walked over and looked at them. He was smiling, until he saw mine.

'Whose is this?' he asked, pointing at mine.

'Mine,' I said very quietly.

'It looks absolutely rubbish.' He turned to Mrs Moritz. 'Just put this one in the bin,' he said.

Mrs Moritz stood up and looked fierce. 'Mr Winters, you should be ashamed of yourself. We want the tiles to represent all abilities. Not everyone can write neatly. At least she had a go. I've a good mind to report you for discrimination.'

Mr Winters was fuming for the rest of the day.

Sunday, January 19th

OPERATION ROLLER SKATES

This morning I covered the roller skates in white paint. I thought they would look better but they actually looked worse. My next idea was to wear large trousers so I sneaked into Dad's cupboard and found a pair of old flares. I tried them on. They were very big and I had to use one of my belts to stop them falling down. Ruffles of material gathered around my feet. The good news is that the trousers will completely cover the skates. I trimmed the extra material off so the bottom of the legs just sat nicely on the ground.

I'm going to look strange but at least no one will see the boots with their buggy wheels and strange white paint. I can't even bring myself to call them roller skates any more.

Monday, January 20th

Bad news! Mr Winters gave me a detention for doing bad handwriting at the museum. It was so unfair. I had to sit in the classroom on my own for the whole of lunchtime play. I watched out of the window as everyone ran around playing statue tig.

'I may be sending a letter to your parents,' said Mr Winters, sighing deeply.

'It was an accident, about the handwriting,' I said. I nearly told him about the cat's cradle when I remembered he'd banned the game.

Even worse, Royalty has slipped into the lead as they got lots of points for good handwriting.

Wednesday, January 22nd

Oh no! When I got home from school today, Mum was standing in the kitchen holding a letter. She had red eyes, which she rubbed when she thought I wasn't looking.

'I've got this letter explaining about your bad behaviour', she said, 'did you really do bad writing on purpose at the museum?'

'Oh, it was just a misunderstanding,' I said breezily.

'I'm afraid the letter also says we're being sent on a course, you and me, a 'parenting for better

behaviour' course. We'll have to go, love. It's in
about three weeks.'

A course? That was a shock. I checked the letter
and sure enough it said that the named child (me)
and a parent (Mum) must meet at Westmore
Community Centre on Saturday, 8th February at ten
a.m. for a one-day course.

I explained to Mum about the cat's cradle tied-up
fingers thing and she thought it was funny.

'Does that mean we can miss the course?' I asked.

'No, we'd better go or I could get into trouble,
darling.'

Oh dear! I'm not looking forward to spending a
Saturday morning with a bunch of out-of-control kids.

Friday, January 24th

I haven't told anyone about the letter or the
course. I'm hoping that I can just go on the day and
no one will ever find out about it. There are a couple
of naughty boys in my class — Jake and Peter. I just
hope they're not bad before the 8th of February. I
would die if they were on the course too.

Today was quite good because it was wet playtime
and we were allowed to play in the hall. We mostly
played wheelbarrow races. Holly and I were pretty
good at it. I'm always the wheelbarrow now.

Sunday, January 26th

I was looking in the local paper at breakfast today.

'Another piece of toast?' asked Mum, but I couldn't answer, I was too busy reading. There was an article about a competition. I remembered back to the old fortune teller at the fair and wondered if this could be my big win. The competition is a National Wheelbarrow Race. This is pretty amazing as we'd only been practising wheelbarrow races on Friday. It was open to teams of two. I can't wait to tell Holly.

'Um, toast, yes please,' I said to Mum, taking the toast as I scanned the article to see what the prize was. It was better than I expected – £500!

Yippee!

The actual race isn't until March but that's good as it gives us loads of time to practise.

Monday, January 27th

I rushed up to Holly in the playground.

'You'll never believe it! There's a National Wheelbarrow Race!' I said, showing her the article.

'Yes, this is it! Your win!' she shrieked.

We practised wheelbarrow races straight away. I forgot the ground was freezing as I dropped down into position. We ran across the playground. My fingers ended up numb with cold.

Tuesday, January 28th

Only four days to go until Holly's roller-skating party. I decided to practise so I put on the roller skates and the large trousers and headed onto the pavement. Joppin ran out after me.

'What on earth are you wearing?' he asked, pointing at my trousers.

'It's fashionable,' I said.

He started laughing and ran inside. I practised for a bit but I was still rubbish. Still, at least the trousers fully covered the skates so no one need ever see them.

Wednesday, January 29th

Number of days until the party = three.

Today after school I was watching TV with Mum. There was an advert for this really good card laminating kit where you make little business cards and put them through a machine to coat them in plastic. It comes with loads of stickers and stamps too. I suggested it as a possible present for Holly. Mum agreed that it looked good and said she'll pick one up tomorrow.

Thursday, January 30th

Number of days until the party = two.

Some exciting news! Holly's actual birthday is on Monday and she's asked me to join her after school for a mini celebration. We're going to an ice cream parlour!! Should be good!

Friday, January 31st

Oh no! The party's tomorrow. I wish I had proper skates. It's so unfair. Mum got the present today and even wrapped it before I got home. Good old Mum.

February

<u>**Saturday, February 1st**</u>

ROLLER-SKATING PARTY AND SLEEPOVER

The roller skates and Dad's flares were in a plastic bag as we set off for Holly's party at St Margaret's Church Hall. I clutched the bag tightly all the way.

'Your friends are going to be jealous when they see your skates,' said Dad.

'Yes,' I replied.

Dad dropped me off at the hall. He said he'd drop off my overnight bag and Holly's present at her house later. He drove off.

I peeked round the door and saw that people were already there. There was a huge mirror ball hanging from the ceiling, causing patterns of light to sweep across the walls as loud music pumped out into the room. Lots of people were skating round, and the sound of wheels on the wooden floor mixed with the music. Some of the boys had scooters but it was mainly modern, beautiful roller skates.

Everyone from our class was invited plus Holly's cousins and five friends from other schools.

Holly saw me and skated over.

'Isn't it great,' she said, bending down to rub a tiny mark off her white-and-pink skates.

'Yep,' I said, entering the hall and looking around the room.

There was a small ramp in the middle and Jake and Peter were taking it in turns to do jumps on their scooters.

'Go and change into your skates,' said Holly with a big grin on her face, 'then we can work on a routine, and then later in the party we can perform it for everyone.'

I scurried off to the toilet and sat down. I could have quite happily stayed there in the loo for the whole party. But I knew Holly would be waiting for me. I slowly changed into Dad's flared trousers and the 'skates'. I carefully pulled the trouser fabric around the boots, making sure they were completely covered.

I knew that wearing them out in the real world was much worse than wearing them in my bedroom. At home it seemed possible that I could get away with no one noticing them, but here I knew everyone would ask why I was wearing strange skate-covering trousers. I decided to pretend it was the latest fashion. I knew I'd have to act confident to pull it off. I stood up, took a deep breath, and burst out of the loo.

I skated through the hall, wobbling from side to side. Because my wheels were so big I looked unusually tall and I towered over Holly.

'Are you on stilts?' asked Jake. He pushed me and I shot across the room. Holly skated after me and linked my arm.

'You're very tall. Let's see your skates,' she said, starting to pull at my trousers. I had to think fast. I pretended I'd suddenly lost control of my skates and zoomed off while shouting 'I can't stop.'

Holly caught up with me and we skated round together.

'What are you wearing?' asked Mandy, gracefully gliding over and coming to a stop next to us. We stopped too.

'Oh, um, latest fashion,' I said. 'We need to practise our routine, don't we, Holly?'

Luckily, Holly, Mandy and Sarah were keen to practise and they forgot about my strange appearance for a while.

Sarah and Mandy skated off together. They did a spin at exactly the same time then high-fived. It looked like they'd practised a lot.

Holly and I discussed our plan for a routine. Luckily, it was quite easy. There was even a bit where we stood still and spelt out the word 'party' with our arms (my idea). Unfortunately, the 'p' looked more like an 'f'.

I managed to sort of learn the routine but it was difficult, especially as one of my wheels was feeling a bit loose.

After a while Holly's dad stood on the stage with a microphone. 'It's time for the displays,' he said. 'Who wants to go first?' Mandy and Sarah put their arms in the air and Holly's dad pointed at them. Everyone moved to the edges of the room and watched them expertly zipping around doing spins and jumps. At the end everyone cheered.

Jake and Peter went next. They did three jumps each over the ramp. Everyone cheered. Then it was my and Holly's turn. We skated in a circle and then spelt out 'party'. After that we'd planned to go over the ramp, followed by a final spin and finish. Holly did the ramp first, landed perfectly then stood waiting for me. Everyone in the room was watching. I looked at all the people then at the ramp. I knew I had to do it. I started skating to get some speed up, then, as I hit the start of the ramp, two buggy wheels shot off and rolled across the hall. I fell on my back, my legs in the air and my boots visible to everyone, the remaining buggy wheels spinning. Everyone stared at the ridiculous spectacle. Mandy giggled so much that someone had to get her a chair.

103

'Are you OK?' asked Holly, rushing over. Holly and her mum helped me up and I quickly changed back into my trousers and shoes.

'Wow, those boots were very um... different,' said Mandy.

'At least you're not hurt, that's the main thing,' said Holly's mum, touching my arm.

The rest of the party was a bit of a nightmare because I didn't have skates on and running around the hall when everyone else is skating isn't much fun.

SLEEPOVER

Mandy, Holly, Sarah and I all went back to Holly's for the sleepover. They promised not to mention the skates, although Mandy kept looking at me and laughing, which I think is kind of the same as mentioning them.

We had a party tea, which was nice. There was also a cake in the shape of a roller skate. Seeing it set Mandy off laughing again.

After tea Holly opened her presents. Mandy got her a colour-changing lamp. It had a remote control with different coloured buttons, which changed the colour of the light. Holly was really pleased and she put it on straight away. She chose the purple colour. Holly gave Mandy a big hug and said 'thank you' about twenty times.

Sarah got her a musical keyboard that plugs into a computer. Holly squealed with excitement and gave Sarah a long hug.

Then she opened my present. I was pleased because I'd got her a proper present this year. My mum sometimes makes me give home-made presents which is soooooo embarrassing. She took the wrapping paper off then opened the box and tipped out the contents. I couldn't believe what tumbled out of the box. There were some plain white business cards, a pen, a few babyish stickers and a roll of Sellotape (scotch tape). There was also a note in Mum's handwriting. Holly picked it up and read it out.

'Draw what you want on the card, stick a few stickers on it, then laminate it by covering it with Sellotape,' she read.

I felt my cheeks flush bright red. Holly smiled politely then put all the bits back in the box and put it on a shelf.

That night we all slept in Holly's room. I was on an inflatable bed. I didn't sleep well as most of the night I lay awake replaying the moment I fell at the roller disco then remembering the moment when Holly opened her present.

I really, really wish I had normal parents.

Sunday, February 2nd

Mum picked me up this morning. I couldn't speak to her at first. She kept asking me what was wrong.

'The present,' I said eventually.

'Oh yes. Well, I looked at the laminating card kit on the Internet but it was so expensive. I thought I'd make my own. It's just as good.'

'But it's not as good,' I said.

Mum's eyes went red as she stared ahead at the road. 'Maggie, people have too much these days. A simple home-made gift is much better than some junk that costs a fortune.'

We sat in silence for the rest of the journey. My skates and wheels sat in the plastic bag on my knee.

Monday, February 3rd
HOLLY'S ACTUAL BIRTHDAY

After school Holly and I went out for ice cream to celebrate the big day. Her dad pulled up at a café with 'Zeb's Ice Cream Parlour' written in black-and-white stripy letters above the door. Holly's dad dropped us off and we rushed in while he parked the car. Inside there were lots of pink and yellow tables and chairs, and all along one side of the room there were rows of different coloured ice cream. We ran along looking at them all – there was every flavour you can think of, even carrot. There were also twelve different kinds of cones to choose from and millions of different toppings.

'Quick, Maggie, look at this!' squealed Holly, pointing at a dish of dried ants.'

'Ewwwwwwww! Dare you to have that,' I said.

'Noooooo way,' said Holly, laughing.

Holly's dad walked in and asked us if we'd picked yet. I chose chocolate ice cream, a chocolate-dipped cone and chocolate sprinkles. Holly chose mango ice cream, a pink cone and popping candy topping. Holly's dad gave our orders to the lady behind the counter then said that we could pick for him while he popped to the toilet.

We quickly ordered him a carrot ice cream in a liquorish cone with the dried ant topping. When he got back, he stared in horror as we tried to hold back our giggles.

'It's just chocolate sprinkles,' said Holly, winking at me. Her dad had a lick then froze as he realized. He ran back to the toilets with the cone in his hand. He was there for quite a long time and when he got back, the cone was gone. He went up to the lady behind the counter and ordered a strong coffee.

We sat at one of the tables and ate our ice creams. Mine was extremely delicious. I had a lick of Holly's, which tasted very weird.

'A juke box,' said Holly, rushing over to a machine on the wall. Holly's dad gave us money for two songs each so we put on our favourite songs.

Eventually, we had to leave and we sang songs all the way home.

'Hang on a minute,' said Holly, as we pulled up outside my house. 'Thanks for making my birthday so special.' She pushed something into my hand. 'Don't look at this until you get into your house.'

'OK,' I said, 'bye.'

I ran in and went and sat in front of the fire. I opened my hand. In it was a small white card carefully covered in Sellotape. On it was written 'Best Friends Forever' above a sticker of a rabbit with googly eyes.

I smiled as I looked at it and ran upstairs to put it in my special items box.

Saturday, February 8th
BETTER BEHAVIOUR COURSE

Mum took me to the better behaviour course today. She didn't tell Dad because she didn't want him to worry so we pretended we were going to get me some new trousers.

We went into the old community centre and were led to a room that was full of mums, dads and kids. I looked at the kids – something didn't seem right. All the children looked really young – two or three years old. They were tiny, naughty kids who kept toddling around and pushing each other.

'I think we've got the wrong room,' said Mum, as a tiny boy hit her on the bottom with a wooden spoon.

'No, this is the better behaviour course. Hello, I'm Mrs Murray,' said an enormous woman.

We sat in a corner on our own but we were then told we had to sit in a circle and we ended up next to two little boys.

'These are the terrible twins,' said their mum, as one pulled the other's hair.

'Lovely,' we said, as they started fighting.

We all had to introduce ourselves first and then Mrs Murray announced we were going to start our first activity.

'I want you all to think of an animal,' she said.

We went round the circle with each child saying an animal's name. It turned out that the same animal couldn't be mentioned more than once, and as I was the last in the circle I was struggling to think of any animal that hadn't been said.

'Rat,' I said in desperation.

'Great. Now we're going to go round the circle and hear what your animal sounds like,' said Mrs Murray.

We went round the circle again and heard a dog barking, a lion roaring, a cow mooing, and almost any other animal you can think of making its noise. It sounded terrible and it seemed to take forever. I went red and did a feeble rat squeak at the end. We then had to go round again acting out our animal's movements. How I wished I hadn't picked rat! I did a sort of burrowing movement with my arms, much to the terrible twins' amusement.

After that we were given a small drum each and we had to hit it as we sang our name and our animal name. Then the mums had to practise saying 'I love you but you must behave well' to the kids. It was mega embarrassing.

We had a good laugh about it on the way home though.

<u>Monday, February 10th</u>
BUDDY DAY

'You are a role model for your buddy,' said Mr Winters. 'I want you to each give your buddy one piece of advice about life. Anyone got any ideas?'

Jake shot his hand up.

'Jake?'

'Umm, my advice is that it's easy to push into the lunch queue if you crawl under the bit the trays slide along.'

Mr Winters sighed. 'Anyone else?'

'Always be prepared for a test,' said Sarah.

'That's more like it,' said Mr Winters, putting a point on Royalty's score sheet. 'Write down your words of wisdom and I'll check them before you tell them to your buddies this afternoon.'

I sat for ages trying to think of something. Holly wrote 'Be kind to people and play with someone if they are on their own.' Mandy wrote 'Always have dangly things hanging off your bag.'

In the end I wrote 'Be yourself.' It was something Mum always said to me.

Mr Winters checked them and said all of ours were good. Quentin had to change his from 'If you can't win, cheat' to 'If you can't win, try harder.'

Hmmmm.

Peter was sent out for writing 'Don't wee around the toilet, wee in the toilet.' I don't see the problem with that, it seems like good advice to me.

Anyway, after lunch we all went to the reception playground and all the little kids ran up to their buddies, except Riley who hid. I eventually saw him standing behind a tree. I walked up to him and stood in front of the tree. I saw Mr Winters watching me so I decided to say my piece of advice.

'Be yourself!' I shouted, just to be sure Mr Winters would hear.

Slowly, Riley peered round the side of the tree.

'You think I'm someone else?' he asked in a tiny voice.

'No, I'm just saying be yourself.'

'I am, aren't I?' He started to cry then ran away. Mr Winters shook his head slowly then walked off.

A point was removed from the Woodlice poster later that day – totally unfair.

Wednesday, February 12th

A letter came for me today. It was from the National Wheelbarrow Race organizers. It said that Holly and I had a place in the race. I can't believe it! I'm so excited. I rang Holly straight away and she's coming round on Saturday to practise. The race is on the 15th of March in London. Mum is really excited too, and her, Dad and Joppin are coming to watch. Holly thinks her parents and sisters will want to come too.

I told a few people at school and by lunchtime everyone was talking about it. It got everybody interested in wheelbarrow races and loads of people were doing it even though it was snowing.

Jake and Peter wanted to race Holly and me but I told them I would be practising indoors so as to protect my hands ready for the real race.

Saturday, February 15th

I put the letter from the National Wheelbarrow Race organizers on the table and Holly screamed with excitement when she saw it. We decided to practise straight away and we went up and down the lounge about twenty times.

The race is going to be at a London racetrack. We looked up the track on the Internet and it was a large oval running track with an orange rubbery surface. We decided I might need gloves for the race and, luckily, Dad had some black rubber ones that seemed to do the trick.

We practised a bit outside but it was hard on the pavement. Even through the gloves the floor felt rough and hard.

After our practising my arms were aching. I could hardly lift my forkfuls of spaghetti at teatime.

'We've got to have special outfits,' Holly announced, as we tucked into our chocolate cake. We decided to make special T-shirts. Holly said she had some fabric paints and Mum said she'd get us some plain T-shirts off eBay. We spent the rest of the afternoon planning our designs. We tried to think of a team name. Combining the letters of our names, we came up with Moggly and Haglie, neither of which sounded quite right.

'I know,' said Holly, 'Wheelbarrow Queens.' I looked at her and smiled. We rushed to my desk for pens and paper and designed the T-shirts.

It's four weeks until the race so we have quite a long time to practise. Dad even said he'd take us to a local racetrack so we could have a go on a surface similar to the one in the real race.

Monday, February 17th

It's all arranged. I'm going to Holly's next Saturday and we'll make the T-shirts and practise in her garden.

Things are looking good. With all this practising there's a good chance we'll win and walk away with £500. Could this turn out to be my big win? I've got a feeling it might.

BUDDY

We went into the reception playground today. Riley ran away when he saw me so we taught some of the other little kids how to do wheelbarrow races.

Wednesday, February 19th

There was a large crowd around the school gates today. I went over to see what was going on. There was a van with 'Barry the Elephant' painted on the side parked right by the school.

Barry the Elephant is this silly kids' show where someone dresses up as an elephant and tries to hide from people. He always hides behind very small things and is easy to see – that's the joke of the show.

Everyone at our school, except perhaps the youngest kids, is too old for Barry the Elephant so no one knew why the van was there.

'Barry the Elephant is so babyish,' said Mandy, running up behind me.

'My sister Bobo likes it but she's only two,' said Sarah, following her.

People were looking through the van window but it seemed to be empty.

We went into our class, everyone talking about Barry.

'Peter loves Barry,' jeered Jake.

'No, I don't, I'm not a baby,' said Peter. There was nearly a fight.

'Barry the Elephant is pathetic and silly,' said Quentin. 'My Mum says that watching it makes toddlers stupid.'

'Oh, you watched it then?' asked Mandy.

Mr Winters came in and took the register. 'Now,' he said, once all the names had been ticked off, 'we have a special treat for you today. Please make your way to the hall.' He blew his whistle and the mumbling began. Everyone was trying to guess what it was all about and saying they hoped it was nothing to do with Barry the Elephant.

We went to sit in the hall and then all the kids from the other year groups came in too. After that about thirty really small children aged about two or three came in. I think they were from a local nursery school down the road. As I watched them walking in I was horrified to notice that the terrible twins from the better behaviour course were there. They all sat crossed-legged at the front.

Mrs Foley, the head teacher, walked to the front of the room. 'Good morning, children,' she said.

'Good morning, Mrs Foley. Good morning, everybody,' we all chanted back.

'Oh, have we got a treat for you today,' she said. 'Maggie Moore, could you come to the front please.'

I stared around me, unable to move. Why was I being called up?

'Come on, Maggie,' Mrs Foley said again, looking around for me.

Holly nudged me and I stood up, baffled as to what was going on. Trying not to catch the twins' eyes I made my way to the front and stood next to Mrs Foley. I looked at the sea of children in front of me.

'Oh look, it's the rat!' shouted one of the twins as he pointed at me. Everyone laughed as I cringed.

'Now,' said Mrs Foley, 'Maggie entered a competition for Barry the Elephant to visit our school and guess what? She won.'

My mouth fell open. I racked my brain. I vaguely remembered entering a competition for a holiday to London and I think there was a runner-up prize to do with Barry. Oh no!

'Barry is a twit!' someone shouted from the crowd.

'Now, now, that's enough,' said Mrs Foley. 'Let's have a cheer for Barry the Elephant.'

Barry the Elephant ambled onto the stage and came and stood right next to me. All the nursery and reception kids at the front cheered. Lots of the older kids laughed and a few people booed.

Barry carried a teapot, which he put in front of his face.

'You can't see me now, can you?' he said in a silly voice. He peeked out from behind the teapot and looked at me. 'So, are you a rat?'

'She is!' shouted the twins, and everyone laughed.

I tried to move to the edge of the stage but Barry followed me.

'Let's sing "Twinkle, Twinkle, Little Star",' he said.

I had to sing it with him then he hid behind his teapot a few more time, and then, thank goodness, it was over.

Thursday, February 20th

Everyone's still talking about Barry the Elephant. Generally, people thought it was funny. A few people called me 'rat' today, which was not quite so funny.

Saturday, February 22nd
WHEELBARROW RACE PREPARATIONS

I went to Holly's house today. We had pizza, carrot sticks, and ice cream for lunch then sat down at her big kitchen table to make our T-shirts.

'Do you think that Barry the Elephant was your big win?' asked Holly, as she started painting the 'W' onto one of the T-shirts.

'Oh no,' I replied. 'It was a runner-up prize, which definitely doesn't count as a big win. No, I think the wheelbarrow race prize is the big one, £500!'

I agreed that we'd share the prize and have £250 each. I kind of felt I should have more as I'd found out about it but I couldn't bring myself to suggest it.

'I've decided I'd go on a cruise with my share,' I said. Holly agreed that she would too and we planned our joint trip as we carried on painting.

We finished the T-shirts and then laid them out to dry. They looked pretty good. Once they were dry we planned to sew sequins around the words.

In the afternoon we practised the racing. My arms are getting stronger and I can now carry on being the wheelbarrow for ages. I've decided to do twenty press-ups a day as well as daily wheelbarrow race training. I'm going to be extremely well prepared for the race. We have to win.

Monday, February 24th
BUDDY TIME

When we went into the reception playground today, I was surprised to find all the little kids running up to me.

'It's Maggie, the Barry the Elephant girl!' one shouted.

'Thanks for getting Barry to visit us,' said another.

As I walked around the crowd moved with me. Then I saw Riley pushing through. His hood was up and his long black coat hung past his knees. 'This is my buddy,' he said, walking up to me. I smiled at him and he did a tiny smile back.

In the end I said, 'Let's play tig. Riley's on.' All the kids ran about playing the game. Riley beamed as he chased them.

Thursday, February 27th

We've been practising wheelbarrow racing all week. The ground outside is very cold so we asked Mr

Winters if we could practise inside. He said that as we were training for a national competition we could use the hall at lunchtimes.

Friday, February 28th

Sarah's dad is really into the Internet – he has a blog and everything. Anyway, Sarah's told him about the race and he wants to write about it on his blog.

Holly and I agreed because if Sarah's dad comes, then Sarah can come and watch too. She's going to ask if he can take Mandy as well.

We all jumped about with excitement about our upcoming trip to London.

Saturday, March 1st

Only fourteen days to go until the wheelbarrow race!! Holly was out with her family today so I had to practise with Joppin. He's not very good at holding my feet up though. For some reason he holds them really high in the air and I'm almost doing a handstand as I try and move about. In the end I had to ask Mum to practise with me instead. She held my feet at a better angle but she was really slow moving forward, so it took about five minutes to get across the lounge.

Anyway, I don't need to worry now because I've found a good way to practise on my own. I put my feet on the bed and my hands on the floor then run on the spot with my arms. It seems to work quite well. Well, it did until Joppin came in crying, saying he wanted to do it with me. Mum said I had to play with him so it was back to the bizarre walking handstand. I was more like a lawnmower than a wheelbarrow.

Monday, March 3rd

Holly and I had a proper practice in the hall at lunchtime. It was a relief to have a partner who knew what she was doing.

At the end of lunchtime Mr Winters came into the hall to see how we were getting on.

'Come on then, let's see,' he said, leaning against the piano.

We scuttled up and down the hall as fast as we could.

'Very good,' he said. 'You know, Maggie, it's great that given your leg issues you've found something that you can do with your arms.'

Holly caught my eye and smiled.

'Thank you, Mr Winters,' I mumbled.

'Really good, well done both of you,' he said, leaving the hall.

BUDDY

Riley didn't talk to me much during buddy time but he did walk around next to me. I still had a crowd following me but it was smaller than last week.

'My buddy,' said Riley to the crowd as he pointed at me. In the end I organized a race. Well, I say organized – in fact, I just shouted 'First one to the tree and back is the winner!' and everyone zoomed off.

Wednesday, March 5th

Today we had a quiz about history. We were split up into our teams – Royalty, Mammals and Woodlice. Royalty won! They got ten points for their team and they are now well in the lead.

This is deeply shocking as team Woodlice has always been pretty good.

Quentin gritted his teeth and shook as Mr Winters drew stars on Royalty's poster.

'Don't worry, Mammals and Woodlice,' said Mr Winters. 'There will be another quiz next Wednesday. You can get more points then.'

'What subject will it be on?' asked Quentin.

'Maths,' said Mr Winters. Quentin smiled. At lunchtime Holly, Sarah and Mandy were all celebrating and making up a special Royalty handshake. The Royalty handshake involved a curtsy, a queen's wave, a twirl, and then a very limp-wristed handshake. I desperately wanted to join in but wasn't sure if I'd be allowed to. Also, Quentin was glaring at us.

Friday, March 7th

When I walked through the playground this morning, I heard a voice calling me. I looked round but there was no one there.

'Behind the tree,' said the voice.

I looked behind the tree and there was Quentin.

'What are you doing?' I asked.

'I've got these for you to borrow,' he said. He handed over a plastic bag full of books. 'Don't tell anyone.'

I peered into the bag. 'Maths books?'

'Shhhhhhhh! Just study like mad so we can win next week,' he whispered, before running off.

I carried the bag into class and hid it in the cloakroom. At the end of the day I took it home and put it on the floor next to my bed.

Saturday, March 8th
REAL RACETRACK PRACTICE

Today was pretty exciting because Dad took us to a real racetrack to practise. There were some real runners there who gave us strange looks as were did our wheelbarrow race thing. It was quite easy to do it on the racetrack as the floor was smooth and a bit springy.

We went right round the track twice, which is a total of 800 metres. We were exhausted at the end and we collapsed into a gasping heap.

Sunday, March 9th

After breakfast I went back to my room and had a look at the maths books. They looked pretty

complicated with titles like 'Trigonometry' and 'Algebra in the Real World'. There were eight books all together so I lined them up on my bed to see if there was an easy one.

I was just flicking through 'Geometry and Topology' when Mum walked in. She looked very pleased to see me looking at maths books. I just nodded and said, 'Yes, I love studying maths.'

Once she'd gone I put the maths books away, rested my feet on the bed, and did ten minutes of arm running.

Monday, March 10th

After school Dad called me through into his workshop. I say workshop but really it's a shed in the garden full of old boxes and bits and bobs that Dad uses to make odd things.

'Maggie, Mum told me... about the maths books.'

'Yes?'

'Well, it's fine to study maths but you really need to know how to use your hands and your creative mind. I wondered if you would help me with my next project.'

It turned out that Dad wanted to make a papier-mâché dog. Mum's trying to sell dog coats on eBay and Dad's plan is to make a dog model to put the coats on for the photographs.

I agreed as it sounded quite fun and we started making a dog shape out of wire, ready to cover it with the papier-mâché later.

Joppin was very jealous when he heard about the dog so he's making a koala bear with Dad right now.

Tuesday, March 11th

Getting nervous about the race. We had a good practice at lunchtime though.

Wednesday, March 12th
GOOD NEWS!

Woodlice are doing really well.

Quentin knew every single answer and we are now back in the lead. YIPPEE!

Thursday, March 13th
Two days until the race.

My family, Holly's family, Sarah, her dad and Mandy are coming to the race! We're all staying in a Travelodge near the racetrack tomorrow night. Sooooo exciting!

Friday, March 14th
One day until the race.

(Writing in the hotel! [By the light of the wind-up torch.])

Tonight was brilliant. We all went out for tea in a nearby pub. It was great being there with all my friends. We even had our own table, just us four girls. We had burgers and potato wedges and they even brought our juice in wine glasses. We pretended we were grown-ups.

After tea we went back to the hotel where I am now.

Our family room has two double beds. I'm in with Mum and Joppin's in with Dad. I'm going to imagine winning the race as I go to sleep. I think that will really help.

Saturday, March 15th
RACE DAY

The day didn't start out too well. Joppin and Dad got stuck in the hotel lift while everyone else was having breakfast. That meant we were late getting to the racetrack.

When we got there, I was surprised to see there were hundreds of people in tiered seats around the edge of the large oval track and ten blue-and-white-striped tents lined up along the start line. Everyone went to sit in the audience area except me, Holly and Dad. We went onto the track.

A woman ran over with a clipboard, 'Ohhh, are you Holly and Maggie?'

'Yes.'

'Right, you're in tent three. Just stay in there until you hear the announcement to get ready.'

We found tent three and Holly and me went in while Dad went off to find the others. It was really strange being in a funny tent but we got on with doing our warm-up exercises.

'I wonder why we start from inside a tent?' asked Holly, as she made her body into a star shape before trying to touch her toes.

'Weird, isn't it. I guess they don't want anyone to see the other people in the race.'

Suddenly, there was a loud tannoy announcement.

'The race begins in three minutes. Please could racers remain in their tents until they hear the start buzzer.'

I began to feel nervous as we got into position. It was a very long three minutes and my arms were beginning to ache even before we'd begun.

Then we heard the buzzer.

My heart started beating fast and I felt sweat forming on my forehead. I began to run forward using my hands. We exploded from the tent at high speed. We went as fast as we could, faster than we'd ever gone before. I was gasping and using all my force, and then I looked up. Blood drained from my arms as they came to a stop. We froze on the track. Holly dropped my legs and I fell to the floor. We stared at the other competitors in disbelief. All the other teams were already round at the other side of the track, but in each team one member was in a REAL wheelbarrow with the other one pushing! We could hear the crowd going wild. Shaking, I got up and we ran back to the tent. We stayed in there listening to the cheering as the race ended.

Dad poked his head round the tent door.

'Oh dear,' he said.

We covered our faces with our hands.

'I don't think that was your big win,' whispered Holly.

'No,' I replied.

No one talked about it on the way home.

Monday, March 17th

Everyone rushed up to us at school today, asking how the race went.

'Oh, it was good but we didn't win,' I muttered.

Mr Winters was especially interested, asking about the crowd and the other competitors. We were very vague and hoped everyone would just forget about it.

Wednesday, March 19th

Quentin came up to Holly and me at playtime.

'I Googled your race and saw the YouTube film — hilarious,' he said.

We looked at each other.

'You're bluffing, there's no film,' said Holly.

'Whatever,' said Quentin, before running off laughing.

When I got home, I rushed to the computer and I found a film of the whole thing – all the real wheelbarrows racing out and me running along using my hands, the laughter from the crowds, the moment we realize.

Even more alarming, there had been seven thousand views. Seven thousand people had seen the embarrassing spectacle.

I rang Sarah to ask if her dad had made the film but he said it wasn't anything to do with him. It could have been filmed by anyone in the audience.

Friday, March 21st

Noooooooooooooooooooooo!

Quentin must have spread the word because now everyone at school has seen it. People keep looking at us and laughing. One boy even asked for my autograph.

'Sorry the race didn't work out as planned,' Mr Winters chuckled as he handed out the maths test, which means he must have seen it too.

I checked on YouTube when I got home and the number of views is now up to fifteen thousand.

Joppin was very angry because he wanted to be in a famous YouTube film, so Mum's filming him falling off the sofa right now.

Saturday, March 22nd

Sarah rang me to invite me to her birthday sleepover next weekend. That should be good.

I asked Mum to take me to town to get a present and she agreed. Yesssss! Shopping trip tomorrow.

I also need a new jumper as we're off camping in nine days. Yes, it's our annual Easter holiday camping trip and it will be cold, cold, cold.

Sunday, March 23rd
SHOPPING

I had a lovely day in town. Dad and Joppin went to the camping shop while Mum and I looked at clothes and gifts.

I got Sarah a money box that looked like a big cupcake and some stripy toe socks. Hooray! Proper presents!

For me we got a black-and-white stripy jumper and some white jeans. I have to keep the white jeans a secret as Dad would say they were very impractical, so I won't be taking them camping. I might wear them to Sarah's sleepover though.

<u>Tuesday, March 25th</u>

Oh no! I checked YouTube today – nineteen thousand views. At least we're on holiday next week so I won't have to face anyone at school.

After tea Dad and I did a bit more work on the dog. We added a few more layers of papier-mâché. It's starting to look really good. Just a few more layers to go then we can leave it to dry while we're camping.

<u>Friday, March 28th</u>
LAST DAY OF TERM

During the day we played all sorts of games and, the best news of all, it's been confirmed that Woodlice is in the lead. HOOOORAY! I wish I had someone to make a Woodlice handshake up with. I looked at Quentin and considered asking him, and then I decided against it.

<u>Sunday, March 30th</u>

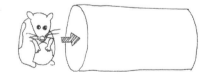

The sleepover party was really good.

Sarah's dad got her a hamster and we spent ages playing with it. We made tunnels out of cardboard tubes and a little house out of an old tissue box. It was soooo cute. I let it run about on my legs. It did do a little poo on my white jeans, which I flicked off quickly.

Tuesday, April 1st
Going camping today.

Thursday, April 10th

Back from camping. It's so nice to be back in my own bed. Coming home is the very best thing about camping.

Sunday, April 13th

Back to school tomorrow. It'll be nice to see my friends but I really hope everyone's forgotten about the wheelbarrow race disaster. I haven't dared look at the YouTube clip again in case the number of views has gone up even more. Might have a peek later in the week.

Monday, April 14th
SCHOOL SCULPTURE

Mrs Foley wants to have a big sculpture in the playground and she needs loads of money to do it, so this Friday the school is having a fundraising day. For £1 we can wear our own clothes instead of school uniform, and we also have to bring doughnuts to sell to each other at Friday playtime. I'm quite looking forward to it and I plan to wear my white jeans and my black-and-white jumper.

BUDDY

Lots of little kids crowded round me again at buddy time. It was starting to get a bit annoying so straight away I said, 'Everyone hide and Riley will find you.' Suddenly, all the kids ran off and disappeared. I managed to come up with a few different games and kept them busy for the whole session.

Tuesday, April 15th

After school I went into the shed with Dad to see how the dog model was coming on.

'Looks really realistic, well, it would if it wasn't the colour of newspaper,' I said, picking it up.

'Wait until it's painted,' said Dad, looking in a cupboard. 'Oh no, I've run out of brown. Could it be a pink dog?' he said, as he took out a tin of bright pink paint.

'No, it's got to look good. It's got to be brown.'

'Well, I'm going to the shops in a week or two. Guess we'll have to wait,' he said, putting the paint tin back.

'I don't want to wait. I want to finish it as soon as possible, plus Mum has started getting Joppin to wear the dog coats for the photographs. It looks ridiculous and no one has bought one yet.'

Thursday, April 17th

Oh no! Holly looked yesterday and apparently our wheelbarrow race film is even more popular now – forty-seven thousand views. Luckily, people at school are not mentioning it so much but it's still very embarrassing to think of all those people laughing at us.

Friday, April 18th
FUNDRAISING DAY

It was funny seeing everyone in their own clothes. Mandy wore stripy tights with a pink dress, Sarah wore blue jeans with a grey T-shirt, Holly wore a long black top with black leggings, and I wore my white jeans and my black-and-white jumper. It was quite a fun day because we didn't do our normal lessons. We did loads of art activities instead. After lunch we went back into our classroom and saw that we were going to be doing painting. There were lots of sheets of paper on each table and on Mr Winters' desk there were five boxes of powder paint. I looked at them and saw that one of the boxes contained brown powder ready for mixing into paint. I immediately thought about the dog. I had this brilliant idea that if I could just get some of the powder, I could mix it with water at home and finish the dog.

I rushed to the toilet and got four blue paper towels from the dispenser. Quickly, before anyone noticed, I put some brown powder paint into the middle of each paper towel and folded them up. I put one parcel in each of my back pockets and one in each of my front pockets. I was very excited about getting home after that.

After school everyone rushed out. Just as I was leaving the playground it started to rain. The rain got heavier and heavier and soon everyone was soaked through.

Suddenly, I remembered the powder paint. I looked down and saw huge brown stains running down the legs of my white jeans. People ran away from me as I walked down the steps outside school. Quentin shouted, 'Uh oh!' and I rushed along as quickly as I could.

Suddenly, a woman came up to me holding a microphone. A man followed her with a video camera.

'Can we talk to you about your YouTube film?' she asked. I stared at her, mortified. I held my bag in front of my legs.

'Um, no comment,' I said, running past them, water dripping off my hair. I scurried home as quickly as possible.

I watched the news tonight. Luckily, I wasn't on it.

Sunday, April 20th

I've been scrubbing my white jeans in the bath but the stains are still there. Oh dear! Looks like they could be ruined.

Monday, April 21st

Quentin was very annoying today. He kept asking me if I'd had an accident on Friday. I said I'd slipped in a muddy puddle.

BUDDY

We had buddy time today and Riley actually held onto the edge of my coat for the whole of playtime. He didn't really say much but everywhere I went he went too. It made playing hopscotch with Holly and Mary very difficult. It almost looked like I was trying to kick him as I did my two-footed jump. I kept a lookout just in case Mr Winters was watching. We couldn't afford to lose any Woodlice points, which could happen if I was spotted kicking a buddy.

Wednesday, April 23rd

When I got home, Dad called me through to the shed.

'Good news, I've got the brown,' he said, handing me a paintbrush.

'It looks really good,' I said, as I started painting it.

We spent a long time on it. It looked really doggish by the end.

'Mum's going to love this,' said Dad.

We're hoping to have it ready by this weekend.

Friday, April 25th

There's quite a lot of grass around the edge of the playground and just behind the tree at the end we saw a wild rabbit. We spent most of playtime waiting by the tree in case it appeared again. It didn't.

Sunday, April 27th

We wrapped the dog up in newspaper and brought it into the lounge.

'Surprise!' we said, as Mum walked in.

'For me?' she asked. We all crowded round as she opened it. When she saw what it was, she smiled and started crying. Dad had even put little wheels on its feet and a lead around its neck as a joke. 'Oh, thank you. It's wonderful.'

'Me and Maggie made it,' said Dad proudly.

'It's marvellous,' said Mum. 'Let's take it out.' She went to get her coat.

'Um, it's for the photographs of the dog coats,' I said.

'Oh yes. It would be good for that too. What a good idea,' said Mum.

We then all had to go the park with a papier-mâché dog rattling along beside us while Mum cried tears of joy. Luckily, I didn't see anyone I knew.

Friday, May 2nd

AMAZING NEWS

'Children,' Mr Winters said, after blowing his whistle three times, 'I have an announcement. On Saturday the 24th of May there will be a charity sleepover at the school.' Everyone cheered and whooped. 'We are raising extra funds for the school playground sculpture. It will cost you £2 each to attend.'

'Where do we sleep?' asked Holly.

'Well,' said Mr Winters, 'we will assign one classroom for girls and one for boys and we will do evening activities all together in the hall.'

'What activities will there be?' asked Sarah.

A mumble erupted in the classroom as everyone started talking about possible ideas. Mr Winters blew his whistle. Then he walked into his little cupboard and reappeared with a box that had been made into a sort of postbox with a slit and the word 'Suggestions' written on it.

We were all very excited and the level of mumbling grew more intense. Mr Winters blew his whistle and the room went quiet again.

'You have a week to post any suggestions for evening activities. We will have a look at them next Friday and see if there are any good ones.'

'I'm going to suggest a scary movie,' said Quentin at playtime. Peter Potter looked worried.

Mandy, Holly, Sarah and I sat at the picnic table in the playground and came up with some ideas. Mandy had this brilliant idea that she'd read about on a website. It's called 'Nail Spinner.' You put different coloured nail varnish pots in a circle with a spinner in the middle. Then everyone takes it in turns to have a spin. Whichever pot is pointed to at the end of your spin is the one you use to paint one nail. The game carries on until everyone has crazy multi-coloured nails.

We wrote the idea down and posted it into the postbox at the end of playtime.

We saw Quentin pushing several pieces of paper into the box straight after us. We decided we'd have to check all the suggestions before next Friday and perhaps remove any unsuitable ones. We don't want to end up doing a load of rubbish activities.

At lunchtime we came up with some more suggestions for the box – hot dogs, hide-and-seek in the dark, truth or dare, and picking up Maltesers with a straw.

Saturday, May 3rd

I asked Mum if I could go to the school sleepover and she said yes. Yippee!

This afternoon I helped Mum take photos of the dog coats on the papier-mâché dog. We wheeled him into the garden and put him next to Mum's lucky tree. She says that if she photographs things next to it, they're much more likely to sell.

Monday, May 5th

Everyone's talking about the school sleepover.

'My mum's getting me a new sleeping bag,' said Mandy. 'It's going to be dark purple with a gold edge.'

I thought about my own sleeping bag, which is light blue with a large rip in it. All the stuffing is splurging out and overall it looks terrible. I'm going to have to ask Mum if she can sew it up before the big day.

Tuesday, May 6th

We put three more suggestions in the box today:

Play dodge ball in the hall.

Do blindfolded makeovers.

Pass an orange around without using hands.

'I'm bringing in the *Haunted Trousers* DVD,' said Quentin, sitting on the edge of our picnic table, 'so you'd better bring in your teddies to hide behind.' He jumped up and did a strange walk as if his trousers were haunted, which was quite funny but we didn't tell him that.

'Well, I might bring in *The Ghoul Butler*,' said Holly.

'Won't scare me,' said Quentin. 'I've got this ability to remain calm at all times,' he said. 'Nothing ever bothers me.'

'But,' said Sarah, 'I don't think Mr Winters is going to let us watch a scary movie anyway.'

Wednesday, May 7th

I showed Mum my ripped sleeping bag today.

'Don't worry, love. I've got just the thing to patch it with,' she said, bundling it behind the sofa. I just hope she doesn't sew anything embarrassing over the rip. I remember once she sewed a baby's sock onto one of my T-shirts. She said it was a money pocket. She even made some 'money pocket' T-shirts for her eBay shop. They didn't sell even though they were photographed next to the lucky tree.

Thursday, May 8th

'We've got to check the suggestion box today,' said Holly just before school started. We all huddled around in a corner of the playground trying to work out how we could do it without being seen.

It was decided that at playtime I would pretend I'd fallen and cut my knee. The others would say they needed to help me, and then we'd all go inside to put a paper towel on the injury. Once inside we'd get the suggestions out of the box and lock ourselves in the toilet to look at them. Then all we'd have to do was pop the good ones back in the box and destroy the bad ones.

Just before playtime I rolled my trouser leg up under the desk and scribbled on my knee with red pen. I rolled my trouser leg back down and I was ready for the plan.

The whole plan went really well and we all ended up locked in the toilet reading the suggestions.

'Watch *Haunted Trousers*,' read Holly. 'Bye,' she added, as she put it in the toilet.

'Oh no,' said Mandy, 'look at this one. See who can pee in a bucket from furthest away. Gross, I bet that's Jake's.' That one also went into the loo.

'Who can eat the most buns competition,' read Holly. 'Hmmm, not bad, we'll keep that one,' she said, making a 'to keep' pile by the sink.

We looked through all the suggestions. There were about thirty altogether. We flushed about twenty down the loo and had ten in the pile to go back in the box.

Suddenly, the bell went. The whole thing had taken a lot longer than expected and the plan to have all the good suggestions back in the box by the end of playtime was no longer possible.

In a panic I put the pile of good suggestions down my trousers, knowing I'd have to get them back in the box before tomorrow.

'Now then,' said Mr Winters, as he sat on his desk. 'I'm off on a training course tomorrow so we are going to look at the suggestions now.'

My mouth went dry as I glanced at Holly. I felt the bits of paper through my trousers. There was nothing I could do. I considered fainting but then Mr Winters might feel the papers as he tried to save me.

He opened the box and looked in. 'It's empty,' he said. 'Have you children got no ideas?'

People started saying that they'd put suggestions in but Mr Winters blew his whistle very loudly for a long time. 'You children have the imagination of slugs,' he said, as he started pacing up and down the classroom. 'OK, I will think of the activities then.'

'But...' said Quentin.

'Quiet!' shouted Mr Winters.

Friday, May 9th

We had Mrs Rizla for lessons today. Most of the time she was out of the room photocopying so everyone was talking about the missing suggestions. People were re-writing theirs and re-posting them.

'I bet Mr Winters hid our suggestions so he could make us do his boring activities,' said Jake. At playtime I managed to sneak the pile of good suggestions back into the box. I just hope he looks at them on Monday.

Monday, May 12th

Mr Winters didn't look in the box today. He said it was too late and we had to learn to do things straight away. Everyone sighed.

BUDDY

We went into the reception playground today to see the buddies. The little kids were all around me again so I told them to all hold hands and run about. I then hid behind a tree.

Tuesday, May 13th

We saw the rabbit again at lunchtime. Mandy said it looked different to the one we saw last time so there might be a few of them. We kept watch all playtime but we only saw it once.

Thursday, May 15th

'Today we have a special visitor,' said Mr Winters after registration. He was standing next to a woman with paint-splattered dungarees and her white hair up in a bun. 'This is Flo Bennett. She will be working with you to come up with ideas for the playground sculpture.'

Flo Bennett stepped forward. 'Hello. It's your playground, so I need you to inspire me with your ideas. The playground sculpture will be large but today I want you to make a small version of what you would like to see out there.'

We were each given a lump of clay. It was quite fun playing with the clay. Holly made a sort of lying-down horse, Mandy made a house (she said that if they made it into a big sculpture, it would be somewhere good to play in at playtime), and Sarah made a sundial. I wasn't sure what to do so I had a go at making a person.

It was starting to look quite good and it actually stood up on its own.

I looked over at Quentin and Jake's table. Quentin had made a snake and Jake's looked like a toilet. Quentin came over. 'I think you hid the sleepover activity suggestions,' he said, pointing a clay-covered finger at me. I just looked at him, unable to speak. He then picked up my sculpture by the head and poked a hole right through the stomach. He put it down and went back to his place.

I looked at my model, which was now completely ruined. The face was all squashed and there was a big hole through the middle. I was just about to roll it all up and start again when Flo Bennett came up behind me.

'Oh my, this is good,' she said, looking at my model. 'I love the distorted expression... and the hole through the middle. That is clever.'

'Oh, thank you,' I muttered, looking over at Quentin who was watching, his face all screwed up.

'It's almost like there's a part of each of us that needs something to fill it up – perhaps community?'

I didn't know what she was talking about but I nodded eagerly. She took several photographs of my piece.

She then went over to Quentin. 'Is it a snake?' she asked.

'Yes,' said Quentin looking at her camera, 'it's a long-nosed vine snake – very rare.'

'It's a bit dull. Try making it seem unusual in some way,' she said, walking off.

I decided not to squash my model after all and I spent some time smoothing the edges of the hole.

Flo took a few photos of other people's models but she kept coming back to mine and looking at it from different angles.

I noticed that Quentin had put a hole through his snake's body. Flo had a look at it then said, 'don't copy Maggie. Try to be original, think of your own ideas.'

I could almost see steam coming out of his ears.

Saturday, May 17th
One week until the school sleepover. EXCITING!

Monday, May 19th
Today Mr Winters told us more about the sleepover. It turns out that everyone will be sleeping on gym mats. The girls will be in our classroom and the boys in another classroom down the corridor. Mr Winters hasn't told us what activities we'll be doing yet but he did mention a maths quiz. Oh dear!

Wednesday, May 21st

It turns out that Mandy isn't the only one who'll have a new sleeping bag for the sleepover. Holly's got one too, a black satin one, and Sarah said she might get a new one as well.

'Can I have a new sleeping bag?' I asked Mum after school.

'Oh no, your blue one will be fine. I'm going to patch it up for you tomorrow,' she said.

Sunday, May 25th

JUST BACK FROM THE SCHOOL SLEEPOVER!

On Saturday afternoon I packed for the sleepover. I took pyjamas, toothbrush, spare clothes, and my sleeping bag. My sleeping bag was all wrapped up with string, but Mum assured me it was patched up so beautifully that no one would notice. She also gave me a packet of biscuits to take, which is quite a surprise as she usually gives me carrot sticks for special events.

I was dropped off at five p.m.

The classroom looked really different as all the desks were in a corner and there were blue gym mats covering the floor. Holly, Sarah and Mandy were already in the classroom.

'Maggie, we've saved you a mat,' said Holly, beckoning me over.

'I'm so excited,' said Mandy, doing a handstand.

Holly, Mandy and Sarah got their new sleeping bags out and laid them on their mats. I decided to get mine out later once it was a bit darker so no one would really notice I had an old one.

'Look what I've got,' said Mandy, pulling a huge bag of sweets out of her bag.

'Yay!' said Holly, pulling a bar of chocolate from her bag. Sarah got out a bag of crisps and I got out my biscuits. We hid them all in Mandy's bag.

We could hear the boys in the classroom next door. I heard Jake shout 'I'm Superman!' Then there was a big crash followed by laughter.

'Hello, girls,' said Mrs Rizla, as she entered the room. 'Is everyone settling in?'

'Yes!' we all shouted.

'Well, it's time to come through to the hall for activities and food.'

We all squealed with excitement as we ran through to the hall.

'Balloons!' we shouted, as we raced in. There were about two hundred balloons bobbing around on the hall floor. Some of the boys were already there, running through the balloons and throwing them about. We ran about playing 'keep the balloons in the air' for a while. Then we had a really nice buffet tea with sandwiches, sausage rolls and chocolate buns.

Quentin came up to us, his plate piled high with sausage rolls. 'Are you ready to be scared later?' he asked.

'Why, did you bring your horror DVD?' asked Holly.

'No, but I've heard that the classroom you're sleeping in is haunted. Thirty years ago a teacher died in there and every night her ghost creeps about.'

'How do you know?' asked Mandy.

'I met this old man outside school yesterday. He told me.'

'You're talking rubbish,' said Mandy.

'Wait and see,' said Quentin, as he stuffed one of MY sausage rolls into his mouth.

'Do you think it's true?' asked Sarah later, her voice wavering a little.

'Of course not,' said Holly.

After the buffet there was a disco. Music boomed out and disco lights started swooping around the room as everyone threw the balloons around. We made up a synchronized dance, which we then did for every song. Jake and Peter did breakdancing and Quentin did a strange robotic dance at the edge of the room.

Later on the girls and I went back to the classroom. Everyone else was still in the hall.

'Hey, we're on our own. Let's muck about while we've got the chance,' said Holly.

She then crawled headfirst into her sleeping bag and stood up. It looked like a huge shiny monster staggering about. Mandy copied her and the two of them waddled around giggling. Keen to join in I untied my sleeping bag. As I unrolled it I saw something that made my whole body go numb. There, sewn over the rip, was a pair of Dad's blue underpants! I looked round to check that no one had seen. Luckily, Mandy and Holly were unable to see anything as their heads were covered by their sleeping bags and Sarah was staring at a times tables poster on the wall. I dived in headfirst and stood up, lunging about trying to grab the others. I plodded about and then I felt a door opening as I fell against it. I went through it and then I banged into someone.

Thinking it must be Mandy or Holly I jumped on her, pinning her to the ground while doing a funny growl. The figure under me started screaming – frantic, terrified screams. I quickly got up and stumbled back through the door. I crawled out of the bag and rolled it up as quickly as I could before anyone saw the underpants. Mandy and Holly came out of their bags too.

'What was that screaming?' asked Holly.

'I think it came from the corridor,' said Mandy, opening the door, but there was no one there. Sarah was still staring at the poster.

'Biscuits?' I asked, trying to change the subject. Luckily, it worked and we tucked into the snacks.

About ten minutes later Quentin and Mr Winters came in. Quentin looked like he'd been crying.

'I think it went in here,' he whispered.

'Has anyone seen a, ummmmm, monster wearing blue underpants?' asked Mr Winters, sighing slightly.

We all shook our heads.

'I need to go home,' whispered Quentin.
Mr Winters led him out and we all looked at each other. Mandy started laughing. 'Quentin's such a baby. I bet he made up that monster story because he's homesick,' she said.

I wondered if I should own up, but that would mean admitting to having underpants sewn onto my sleeping bag so I decided not to.

Mrs Rizla and all the other girls came in. We all took it in turns to brush our teeth and use the toilet, then we settled down in our sleeping bags.

I arranged my sleeping bag so the pants were on the underneath. I don't think anyone saw them.

Mrs Rizla slept in the room with us so we had to have a very quiet midnight feast.

We had breakfast in the hall the next morning. All the boys were talking about Quentin having to go home. Apparently, he was in the corridor on his way to the toilet when a huge blue underpants-wearing monster jumped on him and pushed him to the ground. Quentin had run back into the hall and told everyone but when they went to look in the corridor, there was nothing there.

Monday, May 26th

Good news – the sleepover raised quite a lot of money. This means the building of the sculpture can begin next week.

Quentin was off school today. Peter said it was because of the attack and he's probably going to be off for weeks. Eeeeeek!

Tuesday, May 27th

Quentin's still off school.

When Joppin and I got home from school today, Mum said we couldn't watch TV or go on the computer. She's read an article about how important an outdoor life is for children so we played in the garden, which was actually OK as we found some old water pistols in the shed. I did miss one of my favourite TV shows though, *Bedroom Makeover*.

Wednesday, May 28th

Quentin's still off school.

After school today as part of Mum's outdoor life idea, Mum, Joppin and I went to Potter Bell farm. I'd not been before but it was actually quite good. They have this barn full of hay bales that we played on. There were swinging ropes hanging from the ceiling and tunnels between the bales. After playing in the barn we went on a tractor ride. About twenty people sat in a large trailer attached to the back of a tractor as it rumbled about in a field. It was really bumpy and it kept going through puddles. Quite fun.

In the gift shop I noticed a leaflet for a Potter Bell Birthday Party. I grabbed one, after all it's only six weeks until my birthday.

Monday, June 2nd

'Quentin's back,' said Holly, as I entered the playground today. We joined the crowd that had gathered around him, everyone asking for details about the blue monster.

'It turns out it was a real monster,' he said. 'The police caught it the next day. That's why I've been off school. I've been helping with the police investigation.'

'Wow,' said Jake, 'really?'

'Of course,' replied Quentin, 'and because I'd actually almost won a fight with it they thought I'd be the best person to help.'

Most people walked off shaking their heads but a few of the boys looked impressed and carried on asking questions.

BUDDY

We went to see our buddies today. I hid behind a tree as I was getting fed up of being the centre of attention, but some of the little kids found me and thought I was playing hide-and-seek. I told them it was their turn to hide. They all ran off giggling and I went back behind the tree for the rest of playtime. It was the quietest the playground has ever been.

Wednesday, June 4th

'In one month to celebrate the end of the school year, we will be having a sports day,' announced Mr Winters today. 'You can get extra points for your teams by winning events.' He walked over to the points posters on the wall. 'I see that it is very close between Royalty and Woodlice, but anything could happen, any team could win the big prize.' At playtime Quentin ran over to me.

'You've got to train hard. We've got to win that trip to The Big Apple,' he said, as he started doing star jumps.

Saturday, June 7th

Just in case The Big Apple isn't my big win I looked through the newspaper today. Unfortunately, I couldn't find any good competitions to enter. There was one to win a vegetable peeler, which I decided against.

It's starting to look like the Woodlice trip to The Big Apple (aka New York) is probably going to be the big win. I remembered that the fortune teller said 'You have to make it happen'. I guessed that meant training for the sports day so I jogged up and down the drive a few times and did some stretches.

Monday, June 9th

Flo Bennett, the sculptor, was at school today. She was walking around the playground with a tape measure.

I think she's deciding where the sculpture should go. I can't wait to see it!

Wednesday, June 11th

When we went to into the classroom today, the words 'SPORTS DAY TRAINING' were written in big red letters across the whiteboard.

Mr Winters came in and blew his whistle.

'Preparation is the key to success,' he said. 'Today we will begin our training for the end-of-term sports day.'

We all got changed into our shorts and T-shirts and went out into the playground.

'Because,' began Mr Winters, 'we have someone with medical issues in the class we will be adding some new events to the sports day.'

Everyone looked round wondering who had medical issues.

'Maggie,' he said, 'no running events for you so we have added shuffleboard and 40-metres sideways roll.'

All eyes were on me. I felt the blood rushing to my cheeks.

'I'm OK now,' I said meekly.

'Too risky. You have had serious leg issues recently and I cannot risk you ruining the sports day by getting injured.'

Everyone except me was instructed to run around the edge of the playground. I was told to practise on the shuffleboard in the middle. It turns out that the shuffleboard event involves standing on a piece of wood with wheels on it while pushing yourself along with two walking sticks. So there I stood, pushing myself around the playground. Everyone laughed each time they ran past me.

Friday, June 13th

RABBIT

We saw the rabbit again today. It ran behind the big tree in the playground. Holly's going to bring a carrot in on Monday to see if she can get it to come up to us.

SCULPTURE

Flo Bennett has started building the sculpture. No one's sure what it's going to be like yet but two huge clay feet have appeared on a little hill in the corner of the playground. I've got a feeling it may be based on my little sculpture of a person. YIPPPEEE!

Monday, June 16th

We went behind the tree at playtime and Holly waved the carrot around, hoping the smell would attract the rabbit. It was nearly the end of playtime and we were about to give up when the little brown creature appeared. It stopped quite near us and Holly held out the carrot. The rabbit just stared at Holly so she broke the carrot into two pieces and threw one near it. The little rabbit picked up the carrot and started eating it. It was so cute. We've decided to call it Floppy because of its floppy ears.

The bell went and Floppy ran off. Holly put the other half of the carrot behind the tree in case he came back later.

Wednesday, June 18th

ANOTHER TERRIBLE SPORTS TRAINING DAY

'Maggie, you are practising for the 40-metres sideways roll. Everyone else is doing hurdles,' said Mr Winters this morning.

It turns out that the 40-metres sideways roll involves lying on the floor with your feet tied together then rolling along sideways.

I was extremely embarrassed as I started to roll over and over in the middle of the playground. Everyone else was practising hurdles around the edge.

'Is it a maggot?' shouted Quentin as he ran past.

Friday, June 20th

This morning we had assembly. Mrs Foley, the head teacher, came into the hall holding half a carrot. It looked very like the carrot we'd left for Floppy.

'Someone has been trying to feed the wild rabbits,' she said.

Everyone went very quiet.

'Rabbits are dirty vermin. They are pests and we don't want them in our playground.' She walked back and forth across the stage, the carrot firmly gripped in her hand. 'They eat our plants, they spread germs, and they drop their business everywhere. If I catch anyone trying to feed a rabbit again, they will be severely punished.'

After assembly everyone was talking about rabbits. Some of the younger children with pet rabbits were crying.

At lunchtime we saw Floppy. He looked very thin and a little bit sad. We decided to sneak food in for him on Monday.

'We'll have to be very careful not to get caught,' said Mandy.

Sarah suggested bringing in some of her hamster food. This was deemed to be a very good idea. I just hope Floppy can find some other food to keep him going until Monday.

Sunday, June 22nd

Mum seems to have forgotten all about us not watching TV and I watched the bedroom makeover show with her and Joppin today.

'I wonder if I need new wallpaper,' I said to Mum.

'Oh no, you're lucky, darling, because you have a wonderful room. That wallpaper was £100 a roll, you know.'

Hmmm, looks like I'm going to have to put up with it for now.

Monday, June 23rd
BUDDY

'To celebrate the end of this year's buddy system,' said Mr Winters, 'you will each write a poem. Please include your feelings about your buddy and anything you've learnt from him or her.'

I sat looking at a blank piece of paper for a long time. Worryingly, everyone else was scribbling away.

In the end I wrote:

I guess my buddy is OK,
Although he often hid.
He's playing now and stands near me
More than he ever did.

I was quite pleased with it although everyone else wrote much longer poems. Quentin wrote four pages.

We handed them in.

'I'll make sure the buddies get these before next week,' said Mr Winters.

Oh no! I didn't think the buddies would see the poems. I would've written a much better poem if I'd known that.

Tuesday, June 24th

Today Sarah sneaked in some of her hamster's food in a little plastic box. At playtime I ran behind the tree and poured it on the ground before running away. We then watched from a distance. Eventually, right at the end of playtime, Floppy ran up and ate it. He seems to really like the hamster food, which is strange as it looks so horrible. It's little brown dry pellets with the occasional dry orange bit mixed in. YUCK! Still, he seems to appreciate it.

Wednesday, June 25th

Two weeks until sports day.

We did more training today. Luckily, it was throwing a ball (shot putt) and throwing a stick (javelin), which I was allowed to do.

Mr Winters has written a list of eight sporting events and stuck it on the wall:

100-metres run

800-metres run

Hurdles

Cross-country

Shot putt

Javelin

Sideways roll

Shuffleboard

'Each person must take part in four events,' Mr Winters said after today's training. He walked right up to me. 'Maggie, you can't do any running events so you have to do shot putt, javelin, sideways roll and shuffleboard.'

OH NO!! I'm not very good at throwing things and the shuffleboard and sideways roll training sessions hadn't gone that well.

BUT

No one else practised the shuffleboard or the sideways roll when I did. They were all running around the edge. Hmmmmm, this puts me at an advantage.

Woodlice has to win.

Friday, June 27th

EWWWWWWW YUCK!

A terrible thing happened today. Sarah had brought in the hamster food pellets in the plastic box. She gave it to me to pour out behind the tree.

I'd just taken hold of the box of yucky dried food when Mrs Foley came into the playground. She saw the plastic box in my hand and rushed over.

'What's in there?' she asked, pointing at the box, her face stretched into a growl.

'Umm, my snack,' I said.

'Well, you'd better eat it up then,' she said.
She stood there with her arms folded, glaring at me. I
had to open the box and, YUCK YUCK YUCK, eat the
pellets.

Ewwwwwwwww!

Sunday, June 29th

It's my birthday in exactly two weeks and I'm
having a trip out and a sleepover on July the 12th to
celebrate it. I usually do something joint with Mandy,
(b-day July the 19th), but she's having a theme park
party in the summer instead this year.

My birthday celebration is going start at Potter
Bell farm then we're coming back to mine for a party
tea and a sleepover. Mum even booked us on a
tractor ride at the farm, which will be brilliant.
Holly, Sarah and Mandy are invited.

Monday, June 30th

'You wrote a poem about your buddies last week
and they also wrote a poem about their buddies,'
said Mr Winters, as he waved a pile of papers in the
air. He then proceeded to hand out the poems.

'Well done, Maggie,' he said, as he put Riley's
poem in front of me.

My Buddy

Maggie is a good Buddy.

She is fun.

She got Barry the Elephant to come to school.

The book she wrote for me was good,

And Billy said it was good too.

Thank you, Maggie.

I liked it even though it didn't rhyme and I smiled all day long. We didn't go into the reception playground today though. Mr Winters said we're going to be having an end-of-term buddy party in two weeks instead of weekly visits. I might make Riley a little present.

Tuesday, July 1st

I handed out the invitations today. Only twelve days to go until the party and thirteen days until my birthday.

Wednesday, July 2nd

SPORTS DAY TRAINING

Only one week to go until the sports day.

'You'd better win your races,' Quentin said to me this morning.

Today's training involved me on the shuffleboard and everyone else doing cross-country.

'Please sign up for your chosen events by the end of today,' said Mr Winters once we were back in the classroom. He pointed to eight sheets of paper on the wall, one for each event. I dutifully signed up for my four events.

I wondered who I would be racing against and just before home time I checked the sheets. Everyone (except me) had signed up for the 100-metres run, several people for the longer runs, and quite a few for the throwing events. I looked at the shuffleboard and sideways roll sheets. There was just one person signed up... me.

This is both good and bad. Good in that I will almost certainly win, as long as I can make it to the finish line. Bad because everyone will be watching as I do very embarrassing races on my own.

Friday, July 4th

We sneaked some strawberries in for the rabbits today. We've decided that we'll only bring in food that we don't mind eating if we get caught.

SCULPTURE

Overnight the sculpture overlooking the playground has grown. There are now two huge legs standing on the little hill. It looks quite good but it's going to be very big when it's finished. Quentin's gutted that it's not his snake, and Jake actually kicked the wall when he realized it wasn't a massive toilet.

Saturday, July 5th

'We're doing bar charts at school. I need to know your favourite colour,' said Joppin, as he followed me round the house with a clipboard.

'I don't know,' I replied. I tried to dodge him by locking myself in the toilet.

'I need to know. It's for my homework. What's your favourite flower?' he shouted through the door.

'I don't know.'

'What's your favourite shape?' he asked.

I was getting quite annoyed as I left the toilet and went through to the lounge to watch TV because Joppin was right behind me.

'Stop bugging me,' I said.

'Just a few more questions,' he said.

'Can you ask Mum instead?'

'No, it has to be you. What's your favourite animal?'

I didn't really want to play so I decided to just say 'chicken' as the answer to everything until he got the message and left me alone.

'Chicken,' I said. He eagerly wrote it down.

'Colour?'

'The colour of a chicken,' I said.

'Shape?'

'The shape of a chicken.'

'Flower?'

'The chicken flower.'

'Well, I think that's all the questions,' he said, clutching his clipboard and leaving the room.

I laughed at the thought of my answers being part of his bar charts. It'll probably be a very small bar for the chicken flower.

Sunday, July 6th

Today I made a felt bogeyman toy for Riley. Mum really likes making things and she helped me with the design but I did all the sewing myself. It looks just like the character from the book.

After that I thought I'd better do a bit of practice for the sports day. There was no need to practise for the sideways roll or the shuffleboard so I concentrated on throwing things. I couldn't find anything as heavy as a shot putt or as long as a javelin so I just threw a gold ball and a chopstick across the garden. I couldn't use too much force though as I didn't want it to go over the fence into next-door's garden.

Wednesday, July 9th
SPORTS DAY

There were lots of chairs around the edge of the field next to the school ready for the sports day.

Parents had started sitting down there while the children went into school to change.

It was a sunny day and as soon as we were ready we all ran onto the field in our shorts. I saw Mum and Dad in the second row.

'Maggie!' shouted Mum, as she stood up, waving eagerly.

I gave her a very quick wave then did my warm-up stretches.

There was a loud buzzing noise then Mr Winters' voice echoed out through a megaphone. 'Holly, Claire, Mandy and Mary for the 100-metres sprint.'

They rushed up to the start line, a loud buzzer sounded, and the sports day began.

All the running races were first so I stood at the edge cheering on Mandy, Holly and Sarah.

'Don't cheer the enemy,' hissed Quentin, 'cheer for me and the other Woodlice.'

I was too embarrassed to cheer for Quentin so I carried on cheering for my friends when he wasn't looking.

'Maggie Moore for the sideways roll.' It was Mr Winters' voice, booming loud and distorted through the megaphone. I rushed to the race area. Everyone was watching eagerly. It was very quiet and all eyes were on me. I lay down on at the start line and Mr Winters tied my feet together. The buzzer went and I started to roll. I seemed to be rolling for a very long time. I was dizzy and I could hear hoots of laughter coming from the crowd as the world seemed to tumble around me. Eventually, everyone started cheering, which I took to mean I'd passed the finish line. Mr Winters untied my feet. I got up and staggered off.

'Well done, Maggie, first place,' said Mr Winters, patting my back.

I'm not sure that first place in a race for one is anything to be proud of but still, it's a point for Woodlice.

'Good race,' said Quentin, his shoulders shaking up and down. 'Still, at least you won.' He turned round then laughed.

Then there were the throwing events. I came last. I was just looking for Holly when there was another announcement.

'Maggie Moore for the shuffleboard.'

I went up to the start line, again on my own. The board was there with the two walking sticks next to it. I picked them up and stood on the board.

'Go, Maggie!' shouted Mum from the audience. Then the buzzer sounded. It was at that moment that I found I had a major problem. When I'd been practising the shuffleboard on the hard concrete playground, it had been quite easy. On the thick grass it was very difficult to get going at all. With each push of the walking stick I only moved a few centimetres. This meant my one race took about twenty agonizing minutes. I was flushed and I couldn't look at the crowd although I could hear them shouting 'Come on!' Eventually, I reached the finish line and got first place.

Thursday, July 10th
HOORAY FOR WOODLICE!

When we got to school today, Mr Winters was adding stars to our team posters. It looked quite close between Royalty and Woodlice and I was feeling a bit worried.

Once we'd all sat down he added a last star to Woodlice and turned round. 'The winning team is Woodlice,' he said. All the Woodlice, including me, cheered. 'Here is a letter for your parents about the trip.'

I was so excited I could hardly hold my letter still. I gave it a quick read.

Dear Parent / Guardian,

We have been running a good work reward scheme at school this year and your child was on the winning team. As a reward, we will be taking the said child on a surprise trip on Friday, 18th July. Please check your emails for further details.

YIPPEE!

YIPPEE!

It's a shame none of my friends are coming but still, the Big Apple, New York!

Sooooooooooooooo excited!

After school I told Mum all about the trip to America and gave her the letter.

'It doesn't say anything about America, love. I think it's a day trip,' she said, after she'd checked her emails.

'No, no, it's definitely America. I'll check tomorrow,' I replied.

Friday, July 11th

'Quentin,' I said, when I entered the playground today, 'my mum said that the email didn't mention America but I'm sure The Big Apple is another name for New York. Do you know?'

'Yeah, yeah, it is America but the email told parents to keep it a secret so it'll be a surprise for the children,' he said.

'I knew it,' I said.

'Just pack loads and loads of stuff,' said Quentin.

I was so excited all day. Mandy kept telling me about her American holiday. The shops, the cafes and the big buildings sound amazing. I hope I get to go shopping and pick up some rubbers for my collection.

ROOM MAKEOVER

I don't know for sure what's going on but I think Dad might be taking my horrible flowery wallpaper down.

When I got home, there was a big sign on my bedroom door that said 'NO ENTRY – SURPRISE IN PROGRESS'. Hooray! My room might actually look good for the sleepover tomorrow night.

'You'll have to sleep in Joppin's room tonight,' said Mum at tea time, 'while Dad finishes your birthday surprise.'

I didn't really want to sleep in Joppin's room but I decided I'd better let Dad finish the job. EXCITING!

Saturday, July 12th

A.M.

Joppin's snoring woke me up early and I crawled out of the blue sleeping bag.

I went to investigate my newly-decorated room but Dad had put a large wooden bar across the door so I couldn't get in.

The reveal

After breakfast we all stood by my door. Dad took the wooden bar off and swung the door open.

'Surprise!' he shouted. I peered into the room and just stared, my mouth hanging open. The flowery wallpaper was gone but in its place was new

183

wallpaper covered in pictures of CHICKENS!!

I couldn't speak as I looked around the room. As well as the wallpaper there was a chicken duvet cover and a framed photograph of a chicken on the wall, its beady eyes staring into the room.

'I can't believe it,' I muttered, my mouth suddenly feeling very dry as I remembered my sleepover was in less than twelve hours.

'Do you love it?' asked Dad.

'So many chickens,' I gasped.

'Yes. Joppin's survey wasn't for school, it was a clever way to find out what you like these days,' said Mum.

Horrified, I ran into the room on my own and shut the door. Me and the chicken in the photo stared at each other, alarmed.

'Well, we'll just leave you to explore your new room,' said Mum through the door. I heard them go downstairs.

Sunday, July 13th

PARTY NEWS

Update on yesterday's party

I met the others at Potter Bell farm and they handed over their presents for me to open later.

I couldn't bring myself to tell them about my chicken-themed bedroom and I was worried about the sleepover part of the party but I had a plan. I'd decided to remove the light bulb from my room and say there was an electrical fault. This would mean the sleepover would be in the dark and no one would see the chickens.

The barn play was good. We spent ages on the rope swings and then we looked at the animals. I rushed past the chickens, trying not to look at them. After that we had the tractor ride. It wasn't quite as good at the last time because the big tractor was broken. This meant we had to take it in turns to go on a very small toy tractor one at a time.

Once home, rather than rushing up to my bedroom, I opened my presents in the lounge. Holly got me a T-shirt with a picture of a chicken on it. I couldn't believe it.

'Oh, thank you,' I said, glancing at Mum.

Mandy got me a canvas bag with... a picture of a chicken on it.

'Thanks, Mandy. It certainly is a very chickeny birthday,' I said.

'Yes,' said Holly, 'your Mum rang us to tell us about your interest in chickens.'

'What?'

'Well, we thought that's why you chose a farm party too, to be near them,' said Holly.

This was tricky. I didn't want to say that I hated chickens or they'd think that I didn't like their presents, but I didn't want to say I liked chickens because I don't. In fact, I have never liked them less.

Sarah handed over her gift. I opened it and, thankfully, it was a really nice blue jewellery box with a gold trim.

'Thanks, Sarah,' I said, so relieved to have a proper present that had nothing to do with chickens. I opened the lid.

'Aaaaaaaaaagh!' I screamed, as a rubber chicken on a spring jumped out.

'Surprise!' said Sarah.

After tea we watched a film then we all went up to my room. I'd already taken out the light bulb so it was very dark. It was actually quite fun putting out the mattress and sleeping bags in the unlit room.

'Why are you all in the dark?' asked Dad, popping his head around the door.

'Oh, um, the light bulb's broken or it could be an electrical fault,' I mumbled. I was confident there was nothing he could do as I'd hidden the spare light bulbs too.

'Don't worry,' said Dad, disappearing.

A few minutes later he came back with four torches.

As the beams of light scanned the room chickens could be seen everywhere.

Mandy gasped in horror then everyone laughed.

'You are strange liking chickens,' said Mandy.

'Sleeping bag monster fight?' I asked, changing the subject.

This morning

BIRTHDAY

'Happy birthday, Maggie,' Holly said from her bed. I opened my eyes to find light streaming in through the window. All the chickens were lit up and they all seemed to be looking at me.

Everyone sang 'Happy Birthday' as we tucked into a pancake and chocolate spread breakfast.

Soon everyone had gone home and it was just me, Mum, Dad and Joppin.

'So,' I said to Mum, 'do I have any um... presents?'

'Oh,' said Mum, looking at Dad, 'well, darling, the bedroom makeover is your present.'

'And I made the framed photo of the chicken,'
added Joppin.

'Thanks,' I said, trying to hide my disappointment.
That night I put the bogeyman doll in my bag then lay
on my bed and tried not to think about chickens.

<u>Monday, July 14th</u>
SCULPTURE

When I got to school today, I was surprised to see
lots of people were on the pavement refusing to go
into the playground where we usually wait before
school.

'It's too freaky,' said Claire.

'I want to be sick,' said Jake.

Holly came up to me. 'Come on, let's go and see
what it is,' she said, linking my arm.

We entered the playground and saw it straight
away. There, on the little hill at the edge of the
playground, was a huge hideous figure with a
squashed face and a hole through its middle. It
looked scary and very strange.

'Hey, it's your design,' said Holly.

'I can't believe it,' I said, a mixture of pride that
my design was chosen and horror at how awful it
looked sweeping through me.

Quentin ran over. 'Hey, my design,' he said,
pointing at the sculpture.

'You only designed the hole,' I said, 'and because the hole is made of nothing you kind of designed nothing.' I was quite proud of my quick thinking.

'Are you all packed for Friday?' Quentin asked.

'Not yet.'

'Well, we're going to be there for a week so pack loads.'

BUDDY PARTY

'To celebrate the end of this year's buddy scheme, the reception children will be coming into our playground for the buddy party,' said Mr Winters.

We got the playground ready by putting snacks on the picnic tables and getting the hula hoops out.

We all waited in the playground. Everyone was talking about the sculpture. Many people were refusing to look at it. Suddenly, Mrs Rizla came through the gate. The thirty reception children followed her.

As they entered the playground many of the children started crying, hiding, and quivering with fear. I couldn't see Riley but I suspected that he was one of the hiders.

Mary, Holly's buddy, was sobbing loudly.

'What's wrong?' asked Mrs Rizla, putting her arm around the little girl. Mary pointed a trembling finger at the sculpture.

Because so many children were scared the party had to be moved into the classroom.

Oh dear!

Once safely inside with the blinds closed Riley ran up to me. He smiled and I smiled back. I got the bogeyman doll out of my pocket and handed it to him. His smile broadened as he took it and hugged it to his chest. He ran off to show his friend.

Wednesday, July 16th

I got out my suitcase and put it on my bed. I was just picking out some T-shirts when Mum came in.

'What are you doing, love?' she asked.

'Oh yes, I'm not supposed to know am I about the trip,' I said.

'The Friday trip?'

'Yes, The... Big Apple.'

'I don't think you'll need all this,' she said, peering into my suitcase.

'Better to be prepared,' I said.

Mum laughed and ruffled my hair before leaving to make tea.

I've packed as much as I can fit in:

Eight T-shirts

Four pairs of jeans

Four jumpers

Three notebooks

Full rubber collection
Two pairs of trainers
Twelve magazines

Thursday, July 17th

One day to go until the big trip!!!!!!

Holly, Sarah and Mandy were all saying how much they would miss me while I was away.

'You're going to miss the last-day-of-term assembly on Monday,' said Holly. 'If you get any certificates, I'll save them for you.'

Mandy gave me a few last tips on American culture and I came home to check my packing.

Friday, July 18th

THE TRIP TO THE BIG APPLE

I dragged my case onto the rickety orange bus. Everyone was looking at it and mumbling away. Strangely, no one else seemed to have a case.

Mr Winters said there were no spare seats so I had to wedge the case between my knees and the back of the seat in front, which was very uncomfortable. Quentin got on and sat next to me and the bus set off.

'Where's your bag?' I asked him.

'Oh, some of the bags were taken earlier,' he replied.

I played 'I spy' with Quentin for a while. I wouldn't normally play with Quentin but as I was trapped in there next to him, I thought I might as well. It was actually quite fun as he found mine very difficult. (S.H.N.T.R) – small hedge near the road.

After quite a long time the bus went off the main roads and started bumping about on country lanes.

'Is this the way to the airport?' I asked Quentin.

'Yes, it's a small airport, just for private planes,' he said.

I watched the fields pass me by as we rattled along. I thought about how different it was going to be in New York.

Suddenly, the bus came to a shuddering stop.

'We're here,' said Mr Winters. I looked out of the window but I couldn't see much, just some trees and fields. I was last off the bus because it took quite a long time to get my case unwedged. 'Come on,' said Mr Winters, marching forward.

We all followed him to a forest area. We pushed our way between trees and scrambled over rocks. It was muddy underfoot and my suitcase wheels were juddering and bashing over tree roots.

I couldn't believe that the airport didn't have a car park.

Then I saw it.

My heart sank.

There, in a small clearing, was a large model of an apple, complete with windows and a door. Along the top in peeling yellow letters were the words 'The Big Apple.'

Everyone squealed with delight when they saw it and rushed inside. Soon they were poking their heads out of the windows and popping up through the chimney.

There was a little playground next to the apple house with swings and a few wooden stepping stones, which soon became covered with children.

Mr Winters came over to me. 'Come on, Maggie, I can push you on the swing if your legs aren't up to it.'

'No, thank you, I'm fine,' I said.

I put my case down and went over to the playground. Quentin ran up to me. 'Can't believe you thought we were going to America. As if,' he laughed.

I went on the swings and swung really high.

Saturday, July 19th

Today is Mandy's birthday. She's not having her party until the holidays (a trip to a theme park party for us four – yippee!). I rang her up to say 'Happy Birthday'.

'I can't believe you've rung me from America!' she said.

'Oh, um, the plane broke down so I'm not there yet,' I said.

Monday, July 21st
LAST DAY OF TERM

The girls were all talking about why I wasn't in New York. In the end I had to tell them about the other, smaller, Big Apple. They found it hilarious.

As a special treat to celebrate the last day of term we were allowed to play board games this morning. We played Scrabble... and I won. (Perhaps that was my big win.)

In the afternoon we had the end-of-term assembly. Loads of certificates were given out. I got one for 'trying hard at sports despite having problems'. Hmmm.

Just before home time Mr Winters gave us a leaflet for a fundraising event happening in the holidays. They're trying to raise money... to have the playground sculpture removed! I'm a bit sad about this but I agree that it looks terrible and removing it is probably the best thing to do.

As the girls and I walked along the pavement outside the school Riley ran up to me. He was holding a red balloon by a string.

'It's for you,' he said, holding out the string. I took it and he ran off.

I proudly walked along holding my balloon.

'Your buddy is so sweet,' said Holly.

Tuesday, July 22nd

FIRST DAY OF THE SUMMER HOLIDAYS

I'm going camping with Mum, Dad and Joppin tomorrow. Luckily, my suitcase is already packed.

Well, it looks like there wasn't a big win for me this year, but at least I've got my friends... and my red balloon.

HAPPY SUMMER
THE END

Also available

Printed in Great Britain
by Amazon.co.uk, Ltd.,
Marston Gate.